PENGUIN CRIME FICTION

THE KILLING OF KATIE STEELSTOCK

Michael Gilbert was born in 1912 and educated at Blundell's School and London University. He served in North Africa and Italy during World War II, after which he joined a firm of solicitors, where he is now a partner. His first novel, *Close Quarters*, was published in 1947, and since then he has written many novels, short stories, plays, and radio and TV scripts. He is a founding member of the Crime Writers' Association. Penguin Books also publishes his *The Empty House, The Night of the Twelfth,* and *Smallbone Deceased.*

Books by Michael Gilbert

THE
KILLING OF
KATIE STEELSTOCK

MICHAEL GILBERT

PENGUIN BOOKS

Penguin Books Ltd, Harmondsworth,
Middlesex, England
Penguin Books, 625 Madison Avenue,
New York, New York 10022, U.S.A.
Penguin Books Australia Ltd, Ringwood,
Victoria, Australia
Penguin Books Canada Limited, 2801 John Street,
Markham, Ontario, Canada L3R 1B4
Penguin Books (N.Z.) Ltd, 182–190 Wairau Road,
Auckland 10, New Zealand

First published in the United States of America by
Harper & Row, Publishers, Inc., 1980
First published in Canada by
Fitzhenry & Whiteside Limited 1980
Published in Penguin Books by arrangement with
Harper & Row, Publishers, Inc., 1981

LIBRARY OF CONGRESS CATALOGING IN PUBLICATION DATA
Gilbert, Michael Francis, 1912–
The killing of Katie Steelstock.
I. Title.
PR6013.I3335K5   1981   823'.914   81-2054
ISBN 0 14 00.5838 9   AACR2

Printed in the United States of America by
George Banta Co., Inc., Harrisonburg, Virginia
Set in Bulmer

THE KILLING OF
KATIE STEELSTOCK

ONE

Jonathan Limbery sang in his thick tenor voice:

> "Es zogen drei Burschen wohl über den Rhein
> Bei einer Frau Wirtin da Kehrten sie ein."

[Eight varied and uncertain trebles repeated]

> "Bei einer Frau Wirtin da Kehrten sie ein."
> "Frau Wirtin hat sie gut Bier und Wein
> Wo hat sir ihr schönes Tochterlein."

"It's very difficult, isn't it?" said Roney Havelock. "I mean, it's difficult enough learning to sing in English, but German!"

"German," said Jonathan, "is the most natural singing language in the world. Look at that last word. Tochterlein. You can really get your tongue round Tochterlein."

"What does it mean, anyway?" said Sim Havelock.

"It means 'darling little daughter.'"

The trebles thought this was funny.

"You mustn't laugh when you sing it at the concert," said Jonathan. "It's a very sad song. It's about three students who crossed the Rhine to visit this inn. They were all in love with the landlady's little daughter."

"Her tockter-line?"

"That's right. Only when they got there she was lying dead in her bed."

"Tough," said Roney. "What did they do?"

"They all go up to have a look at her. The next three verses are solos. You'll have to take one each. The first student said how lovely she looked. The second one said he'd always been in love with her. The third one said he was *still* in love with her."

"That's balmy," said Sim. "You couldn't be in love with a dead girl. What would be the point of it?"

Tim Nurse said, "It sounds a bit soppy to me. One thing, if it's in German no one's going to know what it means. It's quite a decent tune."

"It's gone seven," said Jonathan. "You'd better all be pushing off or you'll be late for your suppers."

The boys, who varied in age from Terry Gonville, nearly fourteen, to Sim Havelock, just gone nine, were disposed around Jonathan's music-cum-writing room. The windows were wide open to a late-August evening of blistering heat. They seemed disinclined to stir. Roney Havelock, who was only eleven but took the lead in most things, said, "Do us the 'Walloping Window Blind,' Jonathan. There's time for that. Just one verse. We'll sing the chorus for you."

Jonathan sighed. Then he plucked a single note from his nickel-plated guitar, a note so deep that it might have come from a bass cello. In repose his face was unattractive. ("Mean eyes, a sour mouth and an obstinate chin," Sally Nurse had said, "yet a lot of people like him." "And a lot of people don't," her father had said.) When he sang he became a different person. He became part of the song,

2

serious or humorous, bold or sentimental. A television cameraman who knew his job would have tracked extra close, to catch every tiny detail in a dead face which came to life in such a startling way.

> "A capital ship for an ocean trip
> Was the Walloping Window Blind
>
> [twank-a-pank].
>
> No wind that blew dismayed her crew
> Or troubled the captain's mind.
> The man at the wheel was made to feel
> Contempt for the winds that blow,
> Though it often appeared, when the gale had cleared,
> That he'd been in his bunk below."

The guitar quickened to a livelier tempo. The treble voices shrilled in unison.

> "Then blow, ye winds—heigh-ho, ye winds,
> A roving we will go—oh.
> We'll stay no more on England's shore,
> So let the music play—ay.
> We'll catch the morning train,
> We'll cross the raging main,
> We'll sail to our love in a boxing glove,
> Ten thousand miles away."

Jonathan produced a final arpeggio on the guitar and Roney said, "Go on. Go on. Next verse. The one about the bosun's mate who was very sedate, yet fond of amusement too—oo."

"It's ten past seven."

"One more verse. Just one," said the boys. "Unless we have one more verse we won't go."

A head poked through the open window and Tony Windle said, "You having trouble with your choir, Johnno?"

"It's a mutiny," said Jonathan. "But I'm not going to yield to force. Come in and help me disperse the mob."

3

Tony climbed through tne window, picked up Sim Have-10ck and deposited him squealing onto the front path. Jonathan was putting away his guitar. He said, "Urchins, the jam session's over. If you behave yourselves you can come again next Friday."

The boys began to disperse reluctantly. Roney was the last to go. He said, "You wouldn't get very far really. Not if you tried to sail in a boxing glove."

"Perhaps it was a boat called the *Boxing Glove.*"

Roney considered the point. He said, "Well, that's one solution I hadn't thought of," and sprinted off after the other boys, who were walking arm in arm down the middle of Belsize Road chanting, "Then blow, ye winds—heigh-ho, ye winds, a roving we will go—oh."

"Roving is something I shan't be doing, not for a day or two," said Tony. "That rancid jackanapes raided *my* car last night."

"What did he do to it?"

"He took away the distributor head."

"I say! Not funny."

"Not funny at all," said Tony. "And if I catch him, I'll try to convince him of it."

"Do you think it was boys? They seemed such kids' tricks. Letting down George Mariner's tires and emptying all the water out of old Vigors' radiator."

"You can blow tires up again and refill a radiator," said Tony gloomily. "I shall have to buy a new distributor head, and the car'll be out of action for days. That's what I came about. I promised to drive Katie to this hop."

"Hasn't she got a car of her own?"

"Certainly. But she's a lazy little slut and always prefers to come in mine. Can I use your blower?"

"Help yourself."

But the telephone produced no answer.

"Hell," said Tony. "Now what am I going to do about that?"

"Borrow my car."

"Hold it. I've got a better plan." Tony climbed back out of the window and held up his hand to stop a young man who was coming up the road on a moped.

He said, "Hold your horses, Sergeant. I've got an official complaint to make. Come in."

Detective Sergeant Ian McCourt, who was young, Scottish and helpful, dismounted and followed him in.

"It's that bloody jackanapes," said Tony. "He's wrecked *my* car now by pinching the distributor head."

"I'd like to hear about that. When did it happen?"

Ian had been born in Inverness, where, as everyone knows, they speak the purest English in the British Isles. It was only an occasional broadening of the consonants and a certain formality in his speech that evidenced his origin.

"I can't tell you exactly when. I brought the car back at about midnight last night and parked it where I always do, at the back of the house."

"That's in Upper Belsize Road."

"Number thirty-four. The other side of the Brickfield Road crossing."

The Sergeant made a note. "When did you find it had been tampered with?"

"When I tried to start it this evening. I didn't need it to get to the station this morning. The chap I share the house with—Billy Gonville—he's got a car too and we take it in turns to ferry each other to the station."

"Then the assumption is that this pairson got at your car between midnight last night and first light this morning."

"I imagine so."

"It's curious, all the same."

"Why?"

"When Mr. Mariner's car and Mr. Vigors' car were interfered with we concluded that it was boys being mischievous. But that hardly fits in with something happening

5

after midnight. Boys wouldn't likely be out at that hour.

"I suppose not. So who is it who's playing these tricks?"

"I would hardly classify them as tricks. Trespass and criminal damage. It's a serious offense."

"It seems so pointless."

"You haird nothing?"

"Nothing at all. There's no reason I should. After all, this joker had only got to hop over the back fence from the lane behind the house, lift the bonnet—there's no bonnet lock, you see—and whip out the distributor head."

"Is your bedroom at the back?"

"It is. But I'm a very sound sleeper."

"Would Mr. Gonville have been home when you got back last night?"

Tony looked surprised and said, "His car was there. I imagine so. In bed and asleep. You don't think he did it, do you? No point really. It means he's going to have to drive me to the station every morning until I can get a new part."

"If we knew why it was being done," said McCourt, "we might have some notion who it was. Well, I must be getting along."

"You wouldn't by any chance be going out through West Hannington?"

"Aye. That's where I was bound for."

"Then could you possibly leave a message for me with Miss Steelstock. I tried ringing her up just now, but either she wasn't at home or maybe she was in her bath."

"I shall be calling on the Manor House. I could leave a message with her mother, if that would do."

"That would do splendidly. Just to tell her that I'm car-less and she'll have to drive herself to the Tennis Club disco."

"I'll do that," said McCourt.

"Now that's a good chap," said Tony when he'd gone.

"Wasted on the police in a dump like Hannington. I must get back and change. Are you coming?"

"I can think of better ways of spending a hot summer evening than plodding around the Memorial Hall with a lot of sweaty girls."

"You have a point," said Tony.

Sergeant McCourt and Sergeant Esdaile constituted at that moment the total detective force of Hannington and District. Normally there were three of them, but Detective Inspector Ray was in Reading Infirmary with supposed peptic ulcers.

Because they were short-handed (for this, McCourt reflected, is the way of the world), their work load had greatly increased. An epidemic of country-house burglaries had broken out, starting in the area of Wallingford and spreading south through Moulsford, Compton and Streatley.

"They're cleaning up the whole area," said Detective Superintendent Farr from Reading, who had been put in charge of the counteroffensive. "And they're just about due in your manor, so keep your eyes open."

Keeping their eyes open had involved patrolling on alternate nights. Which wouldn't have been so bad, said McCourt, yawning, if they had been allowed to sleep on alternate days. However, provided nothing unexpected happened, this was his last official duty for that day. He had to visit each of the three large houses in West Hannington and urge the owners, all of whom would be going to the Tennis Club dance, to leave someone at home if possible and, if not, to leave a television set or a few lights switched on and to lock up securely. Or, better than either of these corny devices, to leave a dog loose in the house.

He tackled the street in reverse, calling first at Group Captain Gonville's house, which was the Old Rectory and lay on the far side of Upper Church Lane. The Group Captain revealed that he and his wife were both going to the dance, but he thought that his bull terrier would keep an eye on things while they were away and would the Sergeant like a drop of Scotch. He, too, liked the Sergeant, as did most of the inhabitants of West Hannington. McCourt refused regretfully. He said that if he had so much as the smallest drink he would fall asleep on his moped.

His next port of call was West Hannington Manor. This was the oldest and largest house in the neighborhood and the most likely target for burglars. It had belonged to Matthew Steelstock, the estate agent, who had broken his neck out hunting, ten years before, leaving a widow with three children: Katie, then fifteen and already beginning to turn male heads; Walter, thirteen; and Peter, six. Matthew Steelstock had been a riotous, fast-living, foul-mouthed man, and since he had left his wife well provided for, she had accepted widowhood without any undue distress. As she often remarked, she had her children.

Of these, Katie was now a first-magnitude star.

Who would have thought she had it in her? An attractive girl, agreed. One who took trouble over her appearance and was never short of boyfriends. But so were a million other girls. Then she had to go up to London and get involved with that photographer. The one who got into trouble afterward with the police. But he certainly took beautiful photographs. Artistic lighting, unexpected angles. And he *said* he had an in with the television companies. Well, people like that would say anything, but in this case there seemed to be some truth in it, because Katie started getting better parts in commercials. Well paid, too. About that time she had acquired an agent. "A very respectable man," said Mrs. Steelstock, "with an office in Covent Garden." She understood he had been to Harrow.

Then came the *Seven O'Clock Show.* The all-family quiz

8

show that combined general knowledge, popular music and a touch of sex. The perfect condiment to season the family evening meal. And starting with one of the supporting parts, Katie had somehow managed to take it over. The producer must have had something to do with it, and the cameramen certainly lent a hand; but it was her own bubbling, self-confident, friendly extrovert personality which turned "Kate" into "our Katie," the two-dimensional friend of a million three-dimensional families; pin-up for a million adolescents; the guest, at the same time real and unreal, at a million supper tables.

"With the money she's made," said Mrs. Steelstock, "she could have gone off and lived up in London with all her smart new friends, but Katie's really a home girl. Her family and her friends are all down here in Hannington and that's where she prefers to stop. We converted the stable block into a self-contained maisonette for her." (If when she said "we" Mrs. Steelstock implied that she had paid for it, this was untrue. The cost of the conversion had come out of Kate's own pocket.) "It gives her just that bit of privacy that all real artists need."

It was Katie's brother Walter who opened the door when Sergeant McCourt rang the bell. He said, "It's quite all right, Sergeant. We're leaving Peter in charge. He's got a headache and won't be coming with Mother and me. Anyway, we'll be back by eleven. We're not night birds."

"That's all right then. And by the by. I've a message for your sister. From Mr. Windle. He won't be able to take her to the dance. Some joker's put his car out of action."

"I suppose it's the same kids who damaged the other cars."

"We're not so sure about kids. It transpires that this incident must have taken place in the early hours of the morning."

Walter considered this slowly. He liked to consider

9

things slowly. He said, "If an adult is responsible, the whole thing seems rather pointless, doesn't it? Unless he has a particular grudge against the three people concerned. Mariner, Vigors and Windle. There doesn't seem to be much connection."

"It's a problem we're working on. I'll have to be on my way. You won't forget to tell your sister."

"That's all right. She'll take her own car, I've no doubt.'

"Or maybe she'll walk."

"Not our Katie," said Walter.

One of the reasons that McCourt had taken a circular route into West Hannington was that it was an excuse for leaving the Mariners to the last.

George Mariner had built the Croft when he came to West Hannington twenty years before. It had taken a lot of money, and the sacking of one architect, to get it exactly as he wanted it, which was odd, because it was not a house of any particular character.

McCourt raised the heavy brass dolphin door knocker and let it fall with a thud upon the heavy oak-paneled door.

When nothing happened, he said something under his breath, knocked again and pressed the bell. This did produce results. Lights came on in the wrought-iron lanterns on either side of the porch and the door was opened by a smart-looking maid.

McCourt said, "Is Mr. Mariner in?"

The maid said, in tones which would have suited a fifty-year-old butler, "I will ascertain if he is at home. May I have your name?"

"Don't be daft, Polly. You know perfectly well who I am. Buzz along like a good girl and get hold of him."

"Will you come this way please," said the maid, without abating a jot of her formality. "If you will be good enough to wait." She showed him into the room on the left of the

10

hall, which was George Mariner's study or business room, and departed, closing the door carefully behind her. McCourt sighed and contained his soul in patience. It was a full ten minutes before the master of the house appeared.

"Sorry to keep you waiting, Sergeant," he said amiably. "I was in my bath."

The pinkness and whiteness of his face, the smartness of his lightweight linen suit, the crispness of his shirt reproved the Sergeant, who felt hot, sticky and dirty and illogically blamed this on the cool figure in front of him.

"Can I offer you a drink?"

"Not just now, sir."

"Then you won't object to me having one myself." Mariner turned his broad back on the Sergeant and mixed himself a generous Scotch and water. "Now tell me, what is it brings you out on this hot evening?"

McCourt explained. Mariner said, "Have no fear. My girl will be here until we get back. And even if the house was empty I shouldn't feel uneasy. I have Chubb locks on the front and back door, window locks on all the ground-floor windows and a burglar alarm which sounds off in your police station. I take it there will be someone on duty tonight?"

"Aye," said McCourt. "There'll be a night duty man there. I'll be getting along now."

Mariner touched a bell in the wainscoting and said, "Polly will show you out." He then sat down at his desk, inserted a sheet of paper into the typewriter and started to type, not inexpertly. The Sergeant retired to the hall, where he found the maid waiting. He said, "So you're not going to the dance, Polly?"

"I haven't been asked," said the girl, who seemed to have abandoned her impersonation of Jeeves. "As if I'd want to go anyway. A lot of toffee-nosed crumbs."

McCourt grinned, resisted the temptation to smack the bottom which, in its tight black dress, seemed to be inviting a smack, and clumped out of the door. He said, "Be good, then."

"Not much chance of being anything else in this dump," said Polly. "Tarrah."

She watched him go. She thought he was rather a dish. A bit solemn, but good-looking in a dark Scottish way. A bit like Gregory Peck, really.

At the police station McCourt found Detective Sergeant Esdaile, a Yorkshireman, his senior in years and rank, finishing an accident report. He said, "I've done the West Hannington lot, Eddie. My God, how I hate that man."

"Who?"

"The bloody Master Mariner."

"Oh, him."

"Because God made him a J.P.—"

"Not God, the Lord Chancellor."

"You're wrong, Eddie. He wouldn't accept the honor from a mere menial like the Lord Chancellor. It was a direct gift from the Almighty. It enables him to look upon policemen as supernumerary footmen."

Esdaile grunted, looked at the word he was writing, crossed it out and wrote it again.

"True, he only kept me waiting for ten minutes tonight. Last week, when I called on him about the joker who let down his tires—you'd have fancied he'd had his house burgled and his wife raped, the fuss he was making—"

"You couldn't rape her," said Eddie. "She'd freeze your balls off." He crossed out the second version of the word and scratched his head with the end of the pen.

"—he kept me waiting nearly *twenty* minutes. And when he did come down from whatever it was he was doing he spent another twenty minutes giving me a lecture on the proper performance of my duties."

"He's a bastard in any one of nine languages," said Eddie. "How *do* you spell unconscious?"

Old Mr. Beaumorris sat in the bow window of his cottage on the street. The window was wide open. Through it he observed the life of West Hannington. There was not much happened in the village which escaped him.

He saw the Reverend "Dicky" Bird driving past in his battered Austin, the back of the car stacked with folding chairs, presumably destined for the Memorial Hall. He was glad there were going to be plenty of chairs. Mrs. Havelock came striding past. Must weigh all of twenty stone, he thought. In prime condition, though. She spotted Mr. Beaumorris, drew up, poked her head through the window and boomed, "You coming dancing tonight, Frank?"

"I'll be there. Too old and too stiff to dance, though. I imagine all your brood will be in evidence."

"I've told the three oldest they can come. Roney and Sim will have to stop at home and look after the young ones."

"You must find your children a great comfort."

"Sometimes they're a comfort. Sometimes they're a pain in the neck," said Mrs. Havelock and sailed off up the street like a barquentine with the wind behind it. Mr. Beaumorris smiled. He detested all children.

A quarter past eight. Time to be thinking of moving. He liked to be early at functions. It was too hot for his favorite velvet-collared smoking coat. Instead he would wear the white alpaca jacket, which had belonged to his father. The ends of the trousers could be tucked temporarily into his socks. This would prevent them from getting dirty when he rode, as he planned to do, on his ancient bicycle, to take part in the evening's festivities.

TWO

As was his habit, Mr. Beaumorris annexed the most comfortable chair in the hall, shifted it into the corner and enthroned himself upon it; and as iron filings are drawn to a magnet, the older ladies flocked up and settled around him. Among themselves they said, "Of course, old Frank's a terrible rattle. If you tell him anything it'll be round the village in half an hour." But this did not prevent them spending a great deal of time talking to him.

"We live in troublous times," he said. "Violence, dishonesty, theft and assault. I can't help feeling glad, sometimes, that I'm an old man, with not many years to go."

"I hear this gang broke into Lady Porteous' house at Compton," said Mrs. Havelock. "They ransacked the place from top to bottom."

"Poor Lucretia was in tears about it," said Mrs. Steelstock. "They took *all* the silver. She had a complete set of asparagus servers which had been in the family for more than three hundred years."

This was recognized as being a prestige point for Mrs. Steelstock, as the only person present who knew, and could use, Lady Porteous' Christian name.

"I have a number of precious objects in my own little house," said Mr. Beaumorris. "Many of them I picked up when I was working at the V. and A. Fortunately they are hardly the sort of items to attract the rapacity of a burglar."

14

"I imagine you have some valuable things in your house, Helen."

Helen Mariner swiveled in her chair and stared glassily at Mrs. Havelock. This unnerving mannerism was largely due to deafness. Eventually she thawed sufficiently to say, "I believe we have. I leave all that sort of thing to George."

"I saw that nice policeman going round on his motorcycle," said Mrs. Havelock. "I believe he was warning everyone to lock up very carefully."

At this moment Tony Windle and Katie swirled past to the strains of an old-fashioned waltz. The ladies abandoned burglary for a more congenial topic.

"It's time she got married," said her mother. "It can't be good for her, the rackety life she lives in London."

"I wonder she honors us with her presence," said Mavis Gonville. A life lived in and around R.A.F. messes and married quarters had attuned her to precisely the sort of remark which, without actually being offensive, could be taken in as many different ways as her hearers chose.

"She's a nice unspoilt girl at heart," said Mrs. Havelock.

"Is it true that she gets five hundred letters a week from her admirers?"

"I'm not sure of the exact number. Her agent deals with all that sort of thing."

The gyration of the waltz brought Katie and Tony within range of the battery once more.

"She's got an admirer there," said Mavis.

"Not serious, surely," said Mrs. Havelock. "He can't seriously be considering matrimony. He's got a job with some insurance company, but I don't believe they pay him very much."

"If it's as little as they pay Billy," said Mrs. Gonville, "he certainly couldn't support a wife on it. Billy can't even pay his own bills."

Mr. Beaumorris said, "In my opinion, although of course I'm completely out of touch with the affairs of the young, a much more serious prospect would be our journalistic friend Jonathan Limbery."

This produced a short silence while the four ladies digested the inferences.

"It depends what you mean by serious," said Mrs. Havelock. "If one of my daughters was entangled with that young man I should regard it as extremely serious."

"There was something in it at one time, I believe," said Mrs. Steelstock. "And he used to hang around our house a good deal. But Katie gave him no encouragement, of that I'm sure."

"It went a bit further than that," said Mavis Gonville. "It wasn't just a question of no encouragement. They had a flaming row. And since they were tactless enough to have it in the Tennis Club bar, quite a lot of people heard them having it. I believe you were there, Helen."

Mrs. Mariner rotated again and said, "Was I? I don't think so. I believe my husband was there."

"Ah," said Mr. Beaumorris, "but bear in mind, ladies, *Amantium irae amoris integratio est.*"

"You'll have to translate for us," said Mavis. "We're none of us Latin scholars."

"It is a comment, dear ladies, which is attributed to the Roman poet Terence. It means, roughly, that a lovers' quarrel sometimes signifies the rebirth of love."

"There's a nasty draft from that electric fan," said Mrs. Mariner. "Perhaps you'd be kind enough to turn it away from me, Mr. Beaumorris."

"That's a real hanging jury in the corner," said Tony Windle as he and Katie swirled away. "One old man and four old women."

"Five old women."

"Who do you think they're tearing to pieces?"

"Us, of course. Where's Jonathan?"

"He's not coming."

"Oh. Why?"

Remembering Jonathan's stated opinion about village dances, Tony thought it more tactful to say, "He had a piece to finish for his paper."

"I should have thought it could have waited. That rotten rag of his only comes out once a week. If the piece is for next Thursday he'd have plenty of time, surely."

She sounded put out, Tony thought. "So that's the way the wind's blowing, is it?"

"The same again," said George Mariner. "Vernon?"

"Thank you. It's a gin and tonic."

"Gerry?"

"The same. It's the only possible drink on a night like this."

"Hottest for years," said Vernon Vigors. He was the senior partner in Vigors and Dibden, the only firm of solicitors in Hannington. A thin, dry man in his middle sixties, he seemed to feel the heat less than the florid George Mariner or Group Captain Gerry Gonville, tubby, bald and cheerful and recently retired from the Royal Air Force.

"Put plenty of ice in, Sam," said Mariner. "How's the new job going, Gerry?"

"Better than the last one," said Gerry.

The other two laughed. When Gonville had left the Air Force his first job had been secretary to the Hannington and District Golf Club. The story of his brushes with the lady members had become part of local folklore.

"It involves going up to London four days a week, but this one's a sensible sort of job. I help look after all the appeals for the R.A.F. Benevolent Fund. We collect the money. Our welfare department spends it."

Vigors said, "I'm glad you got the job. Cheers, George."

"Cheers," said Mariner. "And a bloody good cause, too.

Though why we have to leave the care and comfort of Air Force men who've fallen on hard times to a voluntary organization is something I've never understood. Did the Air Force save this country in 1940 or didn't they? They did. All right. Then why can't this futile bloody crowd of old women who call themselves a government use a hundredth—a thousandth—of the money they put into bankrupt bloody shows like car factories that can't make cars and steelworks that can't produce steel and pay the Air Force back something of what we owe them."

"I can tell you the answer to that," said Vigors. "Fifty thousand steelworkers and fifty thousand car workers add up to a hundred thousand votes."

"I was talking to old Playfair the other day," said Gonville. "Jack Playfair. He was one of the squadron leaders in Number Six Group. He's in charge of the Recruit Training Centers at Horsham. He said the first thing these recruits ask about when they come in is money. What's the pay? Any special allowances they can wangle? What about free issues? The next thing is leave. They haven't been inside ten minutes before they're thinking of getting out again."

"The first leave *I* got," said Vigors, "was in 1941. One week in two years."

"It was a bit different during the war," said Mariner. "Though I can't help thinking a year or two of active service would do all these young gentlemen a power of good. Sometimes it makes me sick to look at them. Slouching along, with their hair down to their shoulders and their hands in their pockets. What they need is a sergeant major right behind them with a swagger stick."

"It's not their appearance I mind so much," said Vigors, "as the fact that they know it all. The other day a young fellow in our office—not even qualified, mind you—had the nerve to tell me that he thought we oughtn't to act for a man *because he was dishonest.* I explained to him, quite gently, that it was a solicitor's job to act for people who were in trouble—"

"And that half your clients were crooks anyway."

"Well, not quite half," said Vigors. "It's about time we filled those glasses up again, isn't it? The same again all round, Sam. And have one yourself."

Young Noel Vigors and his wife, Georgie, were one of the few married couples who were dancing together. They were both good performers. Noel was saying, "I saw Dad sloping off into the bar with George Mariner and Gerry Gonville. I bet they're hard at it, yackety-yack, yackety-yack, down with the young, up with the old and what they all did in the war."

"Your father was a gunner, wasn't he?"

"North Africa and Italy. Quite a respectable sort of war. Better than old George, who spent all *his* time in the R.A.S.C. dishing out spam and toilet paper to the troops. Not as good as Gerry, of course. They didn't hand out D.S.O.'s and D.F.C.'s for nothing."

It was odd, thought Georgie, how the precise way in which a man happened to have behaved forty years before still seemed to make such a lot of difference forty years later.

She said, "It's difficult not to agree with some of the things they say. I only wish they wouldn't say them quite so often." She caught sight of the Reverend Bird, who had been cornered by Roseabel Tress and had a glazed look in his eye. She said, "I'll tell you one thing. It never really seems to work if you try too hard with the young. I do believe the current generation are as shy and as fly as any we've ever produced. Look at Dicky Bird. He spends hours every day trying to gain their confidence and organize them and entertain them. But he hasn't persuaded a single one of the boys to sing in his choir."

"Maybe they haven't got voices."

"Then why do nine or ten of them go along once a week to Jonathan's house and sing songs there? They're talking of putting on a concert."

"Perhaps it's because Jonathan never bothers to be nice to anyone except small boys."

"Or maybe it's because he's got a guitar. He's a wizard performer with it."

"Oh? How do you know?"

"Someone told me," said Georgie vaguely.

"You should be out there dancing," said Jack Nurse. "When you're as old as your mother and me you can sit around and watch the others. Not when you're eighteen."

"Nineteen," said Sally automatically. She realized that she ought to be as fond of her father as she had been when she was nine, but she was finding it increasingly difficult to keep it up. "Besides, there's no one worth dancing with."

"Mickey Havelock."

"He's just a kid. And please don't suggest Harvey Maxton. A dance with him isn't a lot different from being mugged."

"It's a pity Peter isn't here," said Mrs. Nurse. "I think he's such a nice boy."

She had one eye on her daughter as she said this, but years of family in-fighting had rendered Sally proof against innuendos of this sort. She simply said, "He's all right, I suppose."

The waltz had finished and the band was striking up a tango.

"I'm not much of a hand at this number," said Billy Gonville, who had come up behind them unseen, "but if you're prepared to chance your arm—"

"Why not," said Sally. "You can only die once."

"Come on, then."

In common with other girls of her age and generation Sally was a much better dancer than most of the boys she met. She had never danced with Billy before. He was light on his feet and had a sense of rhythm, if not much expertise. But there was something more. She sensed—and it was a thing a girl is very rarely mistaken about—that he was interested in her. Nor, thank heaven, did he seem to want to talk.

"Billy's a nice boy," said Mrs. Nurse.

"He's in insurance," said her husband. "That's a good steady job. Not exciting, perhaps, but safe."

"When I was a young girl in India," said Roseabel Tress, "I was much attracted by the doctrines of Brahmanism. Brahma is the supreme being of post-Vedic Hindu mythology. I expect you know about all this, of course. You modern young clergymen are taught to be broad-minded."

"Well—" said the vicar.

"Brahma the Creator, with Vishnu the Preserver and Siva the Destroyer. They form the Trimurti, that is, the great Hindu Triad. An interesting conception."

"Yes indeed."

"I was particularly fascinated by the place they allotted to animals in their pantheistic mythology. The elephant, the tortoise, the bull and the snake. Does it seem absurd to you to worship animals?"

"Lots of people I know worship their dogs," said the vicar. "I think I must go and give my wife a hand. We're just coming up for the coffee break."

The coffee cups and lemonade glasses, the plates which had once contained tiny sandwiches, cakes and croissants and now contained nothing but crumbs, had all been cleared away. Outside it was growing dark. Walter Steelstock said to Lavinia, the oldest of the Havelock girls, "It's very stuffy in here, isn't it. What do you say we go outside and get a breath of fresh air?"

Lavinia looked at him thoughtfully. Walter was supposed to be the steadiest of the three Steelstock children, a nice boy, they said, and a great help to his mother.

"O.K.," she said. "It is a bit hot."

There was a curtained opening on the right-hand side of the stage, which led to the back door of the hall. To the left the path led back to Church Lane. To the right a gate gave directly onto the churchyard.

"Let's sit down for a moment."

It was a black night, with the rind of a new moon just showing over the church tower. The seat was set back between an ancient yew tree and an elaborate tomb. On the headstone of the tomb an angel was poised on one toe, ready to take flight at the sound of the last trump. Walter, as they sat down, slid one arm around the girl in a practiced sort of way. The angel looked disapproving.

Not quite as steady as people make out, thought Lavinia, who was nearly eighteen but not inexperienced. That was pretty smooth.

"There's something I wanted to tell you," said Walter.

"Now's your chance."

"You mustn't laugh at me."

"I'll do my best."

"The fact is, I haven't been able to take my eyes off you all evening. Last time I saw you, I was still thinking of you as a schoolgirl. Now you've changed—did you know it yourself, I wonder?—into someone quite, quite different."

A small shadow moved under the darkness of the yew tree. A twig snapped. Walter swung around and said fiercely, "Who's there? Come out of it."

"The same again, Sam," said Vigors. The round had reached him for the second time. Five drinks had inflated them all, but they were far from drunk.

"The real problem of today," said Mariner, "is mindless violence. The sort of violence that ruins football matches, breaks unoffending shopwindows and wrecks railway carriages. It'd be easier to forgive if there was some point to it."

"Like hijacking and kidnapping, you mean?" said Vigors.

"I don't condone that sort of thing, of course. But the people who do it do at least have an objective."

"Even if it's only money."

"Certainly. But they're *not* doing it because they're bored. And they're *not* doing it because they enjoy violence for its own sake."

"Doing it for kicks. Isn't that the modern expression?" said Gonville. "There was a case in the papers the other day. A girl of fifteen and a boy of twelve—*twelve,* mind you—got their evening's entertainment out of kicking an old woman to death. What can you do with people like that?"

"Half the trouble is our attitude," said Mariner. "The government positively encourages us to be weak-kneed. That White Paper they put out, 'Children in Trouble.' What a load of drip! It's not the children who are in trouble, for God's sake, it's their victims. The women and old people they beat up and rob."

"It's not only the government. The newspapers play the same game."

"Some of them."

"Including," said Vigors, "that outstanding example of progressive pink journalism, the Hannington *Gazette.*"

"You mean the gospel according to Jonathan Limbery,"

said Gonville. "I thought that last article of his was practically contempt of court."

"I read it," said Mariner. His face, which was normally a placid and unrevealing mask, had sharpened into more than mere disapproval. Looking at him, Vigors thought, Something personal there, I fancy. "In my view, for what it's worth, that young man should have been prosecuted. Isn't it a crime to advocate the destruction of our existing institutions by force?"

"Sedition," said Vigors doubtfully. "You'd need a very strong case to carry a jury in these libertarian days."

"It was the savagery of the article that appalled me. The sort of gloating pleasure about the prospect of anybody with more money or position than him having their faces stamped on."

"He's a savage young man," agreed Gonville.

"A few years ago it wouldn't have been so dangerous, because people would have laughed at him. Now one isn't sure any longer."

"One can't be sure of anything these days," said Vigors. "Except that if the price of drink goes up much further we shall all have to take the pledge. Cheers."

"Cheers," said Gonville.

Mariner was still angry. He said, "Mark my words, there could be trouble coming, and if it does come that young man and people like him will be to blame for it."

Noel Vigors was dancing with Katie. He was describing the strategy which had led the firm of Vigors and Dibden to an unexpected decision in their favor in the Reading County Court ("with costs") when Katie said, "I'm sorry, Noel. I've simply got to get out."

"Get out? Where to?"

"Out of this place."

"You're not feeling ill, are you?"

"No. I'm perfectly well. And all I've had to drink tonight is one glass of gin and lime—without much gin in it. Be a dear. I think this dance is nearly over. Steer me close to the door, so that I can slip out the moment it stops."

This was the main entrance and exit of the hall. The inner door led into a small lobby, with a gentlemen's cloakroom on one side and a ladies' cloakroom on the other, and then to the outer door, which gave onto Church Lane.

Noel said, "O.K. If that's what you want." The floor was now crowded. He timed his maneuver with precision, reaching the door as a roll of the drums marked the end of that bout of mixed wrestling. Katie awarded him a quick smile, picked up the bag off the chair beside the door, slipped through the door and was gone.

At least two other people saw her go. One was Tony Windle. The other was Sally Nurse. She never took her eyes off Katie for long. Katie represented her ideal. She admired the way she dressed and she modeled her own appearance unobtrusively on it. She admired the success Katie had made of her career, without much hope that she could do the same. It was selfless admiration, unspoiled by jealousy.

"For goodness' sake, Billy," said Mrs. Gonville. "Get your father out of that bar. He's been there for hours. I don't know why he bothers to come to these dances. It'd be much cheaper and easier for him to do his drinking at home."

"It's time all we oldsters were in bed," agreed Beaumorris. He had not stirred an inch from his chair during the whole evening and had enjoyed himself enormously.

Rosina, the youngest of the three Havelock children present, whirled past with Tony Windle in what they imagined was a Highland schottische.

Mrs. Havelock said, "I left Roney and Sim in charge at

25

home. I tremble to think what they'll have been getting up to." She waved to Roseabel Tress, who wandered up in an absent-minded manner which suggested that her mind was more on Vedic Hindu mythology than on the Tennis Club disco.

"If you're ready to go," said Mrs. Havelock, "I'll give you a lift. I don't suppose the children want to come home yet, but they'll have to do what they're told, for once."

"Very kind of you," said Roseabel, staring around the room. "Very kind." The overhead lights had been dimmed and a zoetrope, operated from the stage, was throwing alternate jets of red and green light across the room. The tempo of the band had quickened to a jungle stomp.

"Quite, quite pagan," murmured Roseabel.

"Like demented traffic lights," said Mrs. Havelock, heaving her bulk out of the chair. "Are you coming, Olivia?"

"Walter will be driving me back," said Mrs. Steelstock. "I expect he'll be here in a moment."

"You're so lucky to have such a reliable child."

Joe Cavey had many jobs. His main one was running the boathouse, seeing that the private boats were looked after and club boats shared out equitably. Another of his jobs was keeping an eye on the Memorial Hall. When it was used for a function, as it was that night, he undertook to see the last people off the premises, to turn off the lighting, to see that all the windows were shut and finally to lock the doors. He exercised a similar guardianship over the Tennis Club premises and ran the bar. He was paid a retainer for these activities and had the use of a cottage which stood at the point where Church Lane ran out onto the towpath.

On this evening, he was standing outside his back door listening to the sounds of dance music coming from the Memorial Hall at the far end of the lane. His own dancing days had been ended by a shell splinter through his right thigh at the crossing of the Santerno River. It had severed an artery and he had been lucky not to bleed to death. Fortunately the medical orderly had known his job and had clapped on a tourniquet in time. Joe could still see the bright red frothy blood which had pumped out at such an alarming speed. He sometimes dreamed about blood. His right leg was stiff and ached in the cold weather.

Mr. Cavey drew on his pipe and blew out a gust of smoke. His wife, who had objected to his smoking in bed, had been dead for fifteen years. He thought of her without regret. He preferred doing for himself. Most of his spare time was spent looking after his back garden, with its rows of early and main-crop potatoes, sprouts, onions and peas. He kept a shotgun in his kitchen and waged ceaseless war on the pigeons.

Out of the corner of his eye he thought he saw black shadows moving across the field beyond his garden hedge. The night was so dark that it was impossible to be certain. Dogs? Too big for dogs and the wrong shape. No. They were human, going fast and keeping low. Boys, he guessed. Or girls. Youngsters certainly. Mr. Cavey removed his pipe and bellowed out in his Army voice, "Oo's that?"

The figures checked for a moment, then accelerated. They seemed to throw themselves at the fence which bordered the towpath. No doubt about it, they were boys. Mr. Cavey heard the sound of ripping cloth.

"Young monkeys," said Mr. Cavey. "One of them'll need a patch in his breeks."

He stood for a few minutes more. The incident had disturbed him. The boys, whoever they might be, were clearly up to no good. Either they had been doing something they should not have been doing, or were intending to do something. Their flight had betrayed their guilt.

Mr. Cavey's mind did not move quickly. But, having

thought the matter through, he came to a conclusion. The only place which concerned him where they could do any mischief was the boathouse. A window had been broken there a month or more ago. The culprit had not been discovered. Nor, now that he came to think of it, had the window been mended. Something must be done about that.

Mr. Cavey knocked out his pipe, leaving it on the window ledge to cool. Then he walked slowly back to his front gate, paused to enjoy the mixed smell of the honeysuckle and night-scented stock, emerged onto the towpath and set out for the boathouse, the bulk of which he could see dimly in the distance against the blackness of the western sky.

THREE

"You three can squeeze into the back," said Mrs. Havelock. "You come in front with me, Roseabel."

"It's very kind of you," said Miss Tress.

"Why have we got to go home?" said Rosina. She was fourteen and it was the first grown-up dance she had been allowed to go to.

"Don't argue with your mother," said Michael. "It's time all little girls were in bed."

"I was only just getting going."

"You were getting going all right," said Lavinia. "Who was that character you were dancing with? It was meant to be an old-fashioned waltz. It looked like all-in wrestling."

"It was Harvey Maxton. As you know very well."

"He's quite a useful rugger player," said Michael.

"He certainly tackled Rosina low."

"It's the new grip," said Rosina. "It's called the bear hug."

"Two minutes more and you *would* have been bare. He almost had your dress off your shoulders."

"Get *in,*" said Mrs. Havelock. "Or walk." The three children climbed aboard mutinously.

Their mother drove as she progressed through life, ponderously but steadily. The scattered lighting of the street ceased opposite West Hannington Manor. A few hundred yards farther on, at the point where Brickfield Road came in on the left, a narrow lane branched off to the right toward the river. The bungalow at the far end, as you approached the towpath, was a sprawling construction called "Heavealong." Here the Havelocks, all eight of them, contrived to lead their ramshackle lives. "Shalimar," the last bungalow, was smaller and neater. In it Roseabel Tress dwelt in lonely state. Both bungalows were built on brick piles and were regularly subject to flooding in the winter.

"Come in and have a cup of tea before you go to bed," said Mrs. Havelock. "Rosina can put the kettle on."

"I always put the kettle on. Why can't Lavinia do it for a change?"

Mrs. Havelock waved a massive arm at her children and they disappeared up the path, still arguing.

"It's very kind of you," said Miss Tress. "I think perhaps I would like a cup of tea." It was always a little daunting, the prospect of going back, particularly on such a dark night, to her empty home. Vishnu the Preserver might be there, but so too might Siva the Destroyer.

"I've had a lot of ups and downs in my life," said Mrs. Havelock, "and I've never known any circumstances where a good strong cup of tea with plenty of sugar in it didn't do me a power of good."

The tea had been made and Mrs. Havelock was on the point of pouring it out when she paused. In the silence they all heard the click of the lock.

"Someone at the kitchen door," said Rosina.

"Burglars," said Lavinia. "Go and see, Mike." Michael was sixteen and big for his age. He got up with a fair assumption of nonchalance and went out. There was scuffling; batlike voices were raised in protest; and he reappeared dragging the nine-year-old Sim by one ear. Roney followed, looking apprehensive.

"What on earth do you think you're doing?" said Mrs. Havelock. "You ought to have been in bed hours ago."

"Well, Mum, you see—"

"And what's happened to Sim's trousers?"

"It was old Cavey shouting at us. It startled us. Sim got caught in the barbed wire."

Roney was a very good-looking boy with an engaging smile which had extracted him from countless tight corners. He switched it on now. His mother seemed far from placated. She said, "It was very naughty of you. You know you were meant to be looking after the babies."

"They were all right," said Roney. "They were asleep. Snoring like anything. We didn't think you'd mind if we went out, just for a short time. After all, you were all enjoying yourselves."

"Well—" said Mrs. Havelock.

"You're letting him wriggle out of it, as usual," said Lavinia. "He ought to be on bread and water for a week."

"We'll talk about it in the morning," said Mrs. Havelock. "Take those trousers off, Sim, and leave them on my work basket. They'll need a patch putting in them."

The boys accepted this as dismissal with a caution. When he was safe in the doorway, with the door open,

Roney said, "You've changed, Lavinia—did you know it yourself? I wonder—into someone *quite, quite* different."

"You little beast," said Lavinia, jumping up. "Just wait till I get hold of you."

Roney slammed the door, and they heard his feet scuttering down the passage.

"It's no good," said Michael. "He'll lock his bedroom door. If you want to do anything to him you'll have to wait till tomorrow."

"It's time someone took him in hand," said Mrs. Havelock. "He ought to be at boarding school, only the fees are so impossible nowadays."

"What exciting lives you do all lead," said Miss Tress wistfully. "I really must be going."

When she got home, she undressed slowly and climbed into her four-poster bed. It was a pity the night was so warm or she might have comforted herself with a hot water bottle. She looked at the bedside table and looked quickly away again.

What a difficult and expensive life Mrs. Havelock must lead. Seven children to feed and clothe and educate. The young ones, she knew, went to the secondary school at Hannington—that sweet little Roney—but the three older children were at Coverdales, the well-known Reading grammar school. A day school, but by no means cheap.

She looked at the bedside table again and her resolution weakened. One of the tablets would surely do no harm. The doctor had warned her. They're strong. Don't start to rely on them. It's much better to sleep naturally if you can.

She took one of the tablets. Might two work quicker? Better not. She was already beginning to feel drowsy when she thought she heard a car start up. It must have been parked actually on the towpath. She listened to it driving away, and as she did so was suddenly shaken by an uncontrollable fit of shuddering. It was as though a powerful electric shock had passed through her body. She reached out a hand, which was shaking so badly that she had some difficulty in unscrewing the top of the bottle, tipped out the tablets onto the bedside table and crammed two of them into her mouth. Her throat was so dry that they choked her. She grabbed the carafe of water that stood on the table and drank directly out of it.

Gradually the tremors ceased. Sleep came down like a gray blanket.

The dancers were thinning out now. The bandleader, looking quickly at his watch, saw that it was five past twelve. With luck, and a bit of stage management, he might bring the thing to an end soon. Then he and the boys could get to bed, which would be a blessing as they had an engagement for the following night, which was a Saturday; and Saturday engagements were always heavy ones. Like his fellow musicians, he worked by day and was beginning to feel the effects of trying to squeeze two jobs into twenty-four hours.

Tony Windle was dancing with a plain girl, a serious performer, whose name he had forgotten. His mind was not on her. He was wondering why Katie had been in such a hurry to get away. And he was wondering where Sally Nurse was. When Katie was not available, he found Sally an agreeable substitute. A self-created substitute. He had often laughed at her for her artless impersonation of Katie. But Sally was a very sweet girl. And where the hell *had* she got to? He was thinking so hard about this that he missed some comment his partner had made.

He said, "Sorry, I didn't get that."

"I said that this band had no real sense of rhythm."

"Perhaps they're getting tired."

Noel Vigors said the same thing to Georgie. "You look quite done up."

"Actually," said Georgie, "I'm feeling a bit sick."

"Sick?"

"Don't panic. I'm not going to *be* sick. I'm just feeling sick. Let's get up to that corner and sit down."

Noel steered her to the chair which had recently been occupied by Mr. Beaumorris. He said, "Do you think it might be . . . ?"

"I think it might. I missed at the weekend."

Noel sat down beside her, slipped an arm through hers and said, "Well. What do you know?"

"Which would you like it to be?"

"A boy, of course. He'll be articled in the firm. Third generation."

"Sometime next century."

"You realize we shall have to shift Dad out. The house is crowded enough now. Which reminds me. He's taken the car. How are we going to get home?"

"Walk, of course."

"Are you sure you can?"

"Fussing already," said Georgie. "A month or two and everything will be back to normal, I expect: 'Do you mind filling the coal scuttle and bringing some logs in. I've simply got to finish reading these papers.' "

Mr. Cavey came in and looked around the hall. About a dozen pairs of youngsters were still dancing. He walked over and said something to the bandleader, who nodded and brought the music to a firm conclusion.

Some of the dancers shouted out, "Encore."

Mr. Cavey was looking for someone in authority. The only person he could see whom he would have classified as belonging to the officer class was Tony Windle. He walked across and said, "I think we ought to finish now, sir. If you don't mind."

Tony said in some surprise, "You're packing us up very

sharp tonight, Joe. It's only a quarter past twelve. You usually give us half an hour's grace."

"I know, sir. But I think the band want to get home."

They were already packing up their instruments. The dancers started to drift slowly toward the door. Tony said, "You haven't seen Billy anywhere, have you?"

"Mr. Gonville? No, sir. I did happen to notice, when I was coming past the parking place, his car wasn't there."

"It's not the sort of car you could miss," agreed Tony. It was a blood-red Austin-Healey frog-eyed Sprite, ten years old and lovingly maintained.

The band had filed out of the back entrance and the last of the dancers could be heard claiming their belongings from the cloakroom.

" 'After the ball was over,' " said Tony. " 'After the break of day. After the dancers leaving. After the skies are gray. Many's the heart is breaking—' What's up, Joe?"

"Well, sir—"

"You've been looking like the ghost of Hamlet's father ever since you came in. George Mariner's driven into a lamppost? Old Mr. Beaumorris has fallen off his bicycle? Mrs. Havelock has run over a chicken?"

"It's not really funny—"

"I'm sure it isn't," said Tony, suddenly quite serious. "What is it?"

"It's our Miss Katie. I found her myself when I went down to check over the boathouse. Someone's smashed her head in."

FOUR

Dr. Farmiloe was on the point of going to bed when the telephone rang. Being a methodical man, he noted the time. It was ten minutes to twelve.

He listened to what the telephone had to say, contributed one "Where?" and one "Right" and replaced the receiver. Without appearing to hurry, but without losing any time, he collected a small black bag, which lived in a cupboard in the hall, opened it and added one or two items to it from a shelf in the cupboard. Then he went out, leaving the front door carefully on the latch, extracted his car from the garage, which occupied the space between his house and the Beaumorris cottage, and drove off.

The whole of this sequence of actions took him less than five minutes. Before he had retired into private practice at West Hannington, he had spent twenty-five years as a police surgeon in the Clerkenwell area of South London.

He saw Cavey standing at the corner where Church Lane ran out onto the towpath. Cavey waved to him to stop and climbed in beside him. "It's two-three hundred yards along," he said. "Just before the boathouse."

"Who found her?"

"I did."

"Then it was you who telephoned Dandridge?"

"That's right. Straightaway I rang him."

The car had bumped on a hundred yards farther before Dr. Farmiloe said, "I suppose there's no doubt she's dead."

"I've seen plenty of dead people in my time," said Cavey. There was a note in his voice which might have been panic, or might have been bravado. "She's dead. No question."

"It's not always easy to be sure," said the doctor. A torchlight waved ahead of them. The doctor brought the car to a halt and climbed out. He said, "Better stay in the car. The less feet trampling about the better."

Cavey seemed glad of the advice. He was clearly more shaken than he chose to appear.

The man behind the torch was Chief Inspector Dandridge, who was, at that time, in charge of the Hannington station. He was a slow, heavy Berkshire man. His real name was Herbert, but people had called him Dan ever since he had joined the Berkshire County Force twenty-five years before. He said, "She's over there, Doctor. In the grass."

The girl was lying face downward, with one arm flung forward, the other arm doubled up under her body. Dr. Farmiloe knelt down beside her. He felt for the pulse in her neck and found nothing. Using his own torch, he examined the back of her head carefully and then shone its light into her wide-open eyes. He did all this quite slowly, because he wanted time to think.

He was in no doubt that Katie was dead. He had been sure of that from the moment he had seen the way she was lying: the disjointed, abandoned sprawl, as though the body, deprived of life, was hugging the ground from which it had come. Then shall the dust return to the earth as it was in the beginning. And the spirit— Yes, what had happened to the spirit of Katie, beloved of millions of people who had seen her picture on the small screen and had built their own image from it? The spirit, said the author of the book of Ecclesiastes, shall return unto God who gave it.

The problem remained.

How was he going to tell Dandridge what to do without upsetting his dignity? Because it was clear that he was out of his depth.

Thinking it out as he got to his feet, he said, "I shan't be able to make a proper examination before it gets light. But there are some things I've got to do at once. It's clearly going to be important to know exactly when she died. I can probably tell you that, but I shall need a bit of space to work in. Could you organize some screens?"

"Screens?" said Dandridge vaguely.

Detective Sergeant Esdaile, who had just arrived on his bicycle, said, "There should be a few screens and posts in the boathouse. They had them up round the Gents' at the regatta."

"Is the boathouse locked?"

"Cavey's got the key."

Hearing his name, Cavey climbed out of the car and shambled forward. He averted his eyes from the thing on the ground. Yes, he had a key of the padlock which held the big sliding doors, but it was back at his cottage.

"If he goes back to fetch it," said the doctor, "he could telephone for help. You're going to need all the hands you can get."

Dandridge turned this over in his mind and then said, "Right. Give McCourt a ring, too. He can get down here quick on his moped. And then get onto Detective Superintendent Farr, at Reading." He pulled out a pocket book and scribbled down the numbers.

"Tell him we've got a case of suspected murder. Will he please contact the Chief Constable and then get here as quickly as he can. After that, you might pack up the dance at the hall. Don't say anything about this, of course. The last thing we want is a lot of people coming down to have a look."

The doctor drew a line with his toe in the dust. "Screens here and here," he said. "And we ought to think about blocking the towpath altogether."

McCourt ignored the telephone as long as he could before stretching out a hand. He listened to Mr. Cavey, said "What?" and "Where?" and then "Right" and tumbled out of bed. By the time he got to the boathouse, progress had been made. Three hessian screens had been put up, one along the edge of the path and one at either end, forming three sides of a square inside which Dr. Farmiloe was at work. A long flex had been run out from the boathouse. The light he was working by was an incongruous string of red, white and blue bulbs which had last been used to adorn the rostrum at the annual regatta. White tapes marked off a further area of grass on each side of the screens.

Sergeant Esdaile said, "Now we've got Ian here, Skipper, couldn't he go and break the news to Mrs. Steelstock?"

Dandridge brought himself back from wherever his thoughts had taken him and said, "Mrs. Steelstock?"

"She'll have to know sometime. It doesn't hardly seem right just to telephone her. Ian's got his moped. He could do it easiest."

"Yes," said Dandridge. He moved across and peered over the top of the screen as though he was hoping that Dr. Farmiloe might have brought Katie back to life. "I suppose that's right. You do that."

McCourt looked as if the job was one he would willingly have refused and started to say something. But Dandridge had retired into the hinterland of his own thoughts and was staring at him blankly as McCourt remounted his moped and bumped off along the towpath. When he reached the corner of River Park Avenue, he noticed that there were lights still on in Heavealong, but that Shalimar was dark. There was a little coolness in the air now and he was glad of it. He was not looking forward to what he had to do.

The front door of the Manor House was opened to him by Walter. He said, "Come in. You were lucky to find me up. The others are in bed. Is there some trouble?"

McCourt told him what had happened. Walter seemed to take in the information with deliberate slowness, absorbing it piece by piece, as though to cushion the shock. He said, "Have we really got to wake Mother up? She's probably just got off to sleep."

"The Superintendent thought she ought to know as soon as possible."

"Then I'd better do it. Peter needn't know until tomorrow."

He had himself well under control, the Sergeant thought. He said, thankfully, "I'll leave you to it, then." He was outside the front door when he heard Mrs. Steelstock cry out. It was a cry of pain and shock. But McCourt, who was an observant young man, detected another note behind the simple anguish: a note of outrage, a note of anger with fate for dealing her a foul blow.

Walter noted it too, and was relieved. He had braced himself for tears and hysteria. He had not expected anger and resolve.

His mother threw a dressing gown over her shoulders, went across to a small davenport in the corner of her bedroom and took out an address book. She said, "I'm going to ring up Philip."

"Now?"

"Of course. At once." She was dialing as she spoke, picking out the numbers unhesitatingly.

When McCourt got back to the boathouse he found that reinforcements had already arrived. Detective Superintendent Farr, the head of the Berkshire C.I.D., was talking to a tall thin civilian whom McCourt placed, after some thought, as Sam Pollock, the Deputy Chief Constable.

"It'll be for the Chief to decide," said Pollock. "But I know what I'd do in his place. I'd get C. One in on the act from the start. No offense intended, Dennis, but this girl's a public character. As soon as the news breaks you'll have the press round your neck."

"Don't mind me," said Farr. "I've got enough on my plate already. So far as I'm concerned, the glory boys can have it and good luck to them."

"There's another thing. Agreed, this could turn out to be a local matter. But then again, it needn't be. The girl lived half her life up in London. There are bound to be inquiries to make up there."

"All right," said Farr. "Like you said, it isn't our decision. I can tell you one thing. Whichever way it goes, our chaps will have to do most of the work." He looked at his watch. "It'll be light in three hours," he said to Dandridge. "We want this section of the towpath blocked off at both ends. Put barricades at the end of Church Lane and River Park Avenue. Leave a man here to keep an eye on things. Right?"

"Right," said Dandridge. He seemed happy to be taking rather than giving orders. "You'd better stay here, Keep." This was to Police Constable Keep, who had been on night duty at the station and looked as though he would have been glad to get back there.

After sprinkling a few more suggestions and commands around, Farr walked back to his Humber and drove off. Dandridge said, "See you keep everyone off. Especially the newspaper boys." He then made for his car. Esdaile picked up his bicycle, which he had propped against the farther

40

wall of the boathouse, and said, "I'll be seeing you."

McCourt thought, it was like the gradual emptying of the stage, the release of tension after the high point of the drama. He was perched on the rail of the landing stage which fronted the boathouse. He felt curiously wide awake.

Constable Keep, who had taken one cautious look over the sacking screen and then turned quickly away again, came across and joined him. McCourt got out a packet of cigarettes and they both lit up.

"Who could have done a thing like that?" said Keep.

"I expect we shall find out soon enough," said McCourt.

They smoked in silence. It was past the dead hour of the night. The pendulum had swung across the midpoint and was climbing toward morning. Soon light would be coming back into the world. A thin curtain of mist was beginning to rise from the water. In the intense stillness, they could hear the small sounds of life moving in the long grass and the bushes which fringed the riverbank. A white shape showed through the mist as a single swan sailed toward them breasting the current with easy strokes.

"Nasty brutes," said Keep. "When I was a kid playing about on the river, I used to be terrified of them. They say they can break a man's arm easy."

"Is that right?" said McCourt. He had no wish to talk. If he had any sense, he thought, he'd have gone back to bed when the top brass left. They were going to be busy enough, in all conscience, when the sun rose.

It was as he was starting to get up that they both saw and heard something else. The growling of a car in low gear. The twin eyes of headlights dimmed by the mist. McCourt said, "I'd better stop them before they come too far."

He walked forward. It was a big black car with the stamp of officialdom on it. As he came up to it the lights flicked on inside and he saw the occupants.

The driver was a young man with a young and solemn face. The passenger, who had opened the door and was climbing out, was a small thick person with white hair and a nose which had been broken and badly set.

McCourt recognized him at once.

FIVE

"My name's Knott," said the newcomer. "Chief Superintendent, C. One. And who are you?"

"McCourt, sir. Sergeant. Hannington C.I.D."

"Give me that torch, Bob." He returned his attention to Ian. "I understand you've got a body for me."

"It's behind those screens."

"Someone's had that much sense." He seemed to be in no hurry to examine the body but shifted the torch, not so that it shone into Ian's eyes but far enough for the side glow to light up his face. He said, "Haven't I seen you before?"

"I was two years at West End Central, under Watts."

"Thought so. Never forget a face. What took you out into the sticks? Looking for quicker promotion, or less work?"

"Neither, sir. My mother had folk in these parts. She wanted to get out of London and wanted me by her."

Knott grunted. He had, as McCourt remembered from the previous occasion on which he had met him, an orchestration of grunts which could mean anything. It was not clear whether this one implied disapproval of a mother who could stand in the way of a promising young man's career in the metropolis or contempt for a young man who could fall in with her wishes.

"When was she found?"

"I'm afraid I don't know, sir. I was in bed and asleep."

"Early to bed and early to rise, eh?"

McCourt said, with a smile, "I hardly got to bed at all last night."

"Then why the hell aren't you in bed now?" The torch shifted slightly. "You're not going to be much use to anyone if you're half asleep, are you? Push off. I'll see you at the station at nine o'clock. Not a minute before." As McCourt turned to go, he added, "And not a minute after."

As soon as he had gone, Knott moved across to the screen and peered over. He shone the torch down for a moment, then switched it off and turned to Constable Keep, who was standing impassively. Having discovered the constable's name, he perched himself on the rail which fenced the side of the boathouse slipway and sat there swinging his short legs. Then he said, "Tell me about yourselves, Keep."

"About ourselves, sir?"

"The Hannington Force."

"Oh. I see. Well, sir, it's not a big station. There's Chief Inspector Dandridge. He's in charge. On the uniformed side we've got Sergeant Bakewell. He's the Station Sergeant. And there're two other constables besides me—Coble and Mustoe. Then on the C.I.D. side we've got Inspector Ray, only he's not there just now, being in hospital at Reading."

"Serious?"

"Stomach ulcers. He's been there a month or more. Under observation."

Knott's grunt implied that he knew better than the doctors exactly what this could signify.

"And then there's Sergeant Esdaile and Sergeant

McCourt. Him you were talking to. And Detective Arnold. He's away with a broken ankle."

Knott sat in silence for some minutes. He seemed to be counting up the numbers and estimating the caliber of the forces at his disposal. He said, "Has the doctor seen her?"

"Oh yes, sir. Dr. Farmiloe was here very quick."

"Farmiloe. Jack Farmiloe?"

"I believe that's his name, sir. He was up in London, doing police work, I understand, before he came down here. You may have met him."

"If he's the Jack Farmiloe I knew," said Knott, "we're in luck. It means that one job at least will have been done properly." He swung himself down onto his feet. "Keep your eyes skinned. We'll have both ends of the path blocked by first light. And if anyone comes past, keep them well away from the screens. *But get their names.* Right?"

"Right," said Keep. He thought, Cheeky bugger. One job at least done right. He, too, had recognized the squat white-haired figure. Charlie Knott, one of the self-appointed stars of the Murder Squad. His picture had been in the papers only that week. A case at Oxford. A man being led into the Magistrates Court by two detectives, with a coat over his head and Charlie Knott close enough behind to get himself into the picture. As per usual.

Knott was examining the boathouse. Solidly constructed out of good materials, it had been built nearly a hundred years before, in the heyday of Thames boating. It would last another hundred years, he thought, *if* it was looked after. But there were signs of deterioration. The paintwork needed redoing, and there was a missing pane of glass in the small door set into the left hand of the big swing doors which guarded the main part of the shed.

Knott shone his torch through and picked out the four-oar skiffs, the tub dinghies, the upended canoes and the lines of oars standing like guardsmen at the back.

The swing doors were fastened with a padlock. The small door was locked, too, with a Yale-type lock. Knott wandered around to the far side and found another door. Beside it a painted notice board said, "Hannington Boating and Aquatic Club. Committee Room." This door also was locked.

He completed his circuit of the building, past the lean-to at the rear, and came out again behind the point where Constable Keep was standing. He said, "Who runs this place?"

"Mr. Cavey, he's the caretaker. He's the one who found her."

"So I heard. What I meant was, who's the boss?"

"That'd be Mr. Mariner. He's the president of the club. Mr. Nurse is secretary."

Knott stood for a moment digesting this information. At the beginning of a case, like a careful hostess at the outset of a party, he liked to memorize names and fit them to faces. He walked back to his car. The driver was lying with his eyes shut. He looked absurdly young.

Knott said, "Wake up, Bob. Take the car back to that pub —the one we telephoned—can't remember the name."

"The Swan," said Sergeant Shilling sleepily.

"Right. Drop our stuff there. Tell them we'll want an early breakfast. Then get round to the station. There'll be someone on night duty. Tell him to get hold of Dandridge. I'll meet him there in half an hour. Then you can go to bed."

"How are you going to get back?"

"When I've finished here, I'll walk. It isn't far. Don't try to turn the car. Back it until you reach the turning we came down. And don't go into the river."

"Do my best," said Shilling.

Knott followed the car as it backed. It was a tricky maneuver in the mist but deftly accomplished. He watched

45

the car turn down Upper Church Lane. The cottage on the corner, which he knew belonged to Mr. Cavey, was in darkness. He wondered about Mr. Cavey. The first person on the scene of a crime was always important. He must find an early opportunity for a word with Mr. Cavey.

Turning about, he walked slowly along the towpath, keeping to the metaled portion in the center. On his right the river ran black under its quilt of curling mist. On his left was a strip of rough grass, backed for the first fifty yards by a barbed-wire fence, and after that by a hedge of what looked like thorn bushes and alder. The sunshine of the past fortnight would have baked everything rock hard. But it would all have to be searched, because it was the path down which Katie Steelstock had walked to her death.

He continued on past the boathouse. Here there was a change. No hedge on the left, but a row of fenced building plots. Then a shed. Then a bungalow—"Shalimar" in Gothic script on the gate—and here was the turning he had expected. River Park Avenue. If he went along it, it must bring him back to the main road. Twenty minutes' brisk walk would get him through West Hannington and back into Hannington town.

It would also restore his circulation and give him time to plan his strategy. He had been long enough at the game to know that the first twenty-four hours could make or mar the outcome.

In this case, the fact that important people were involved had given him a flying start.

Mrs. Steelstock had telephoned her brother, Philip, at twelve forty. Philip Frost was the Deputy Director of Public Prosecutions. He had immediately contacted his friend and professional colleague of long standing, Terence Loftus, Assistant Commissioner of the Metropolitan Police. Two telephone calls had followed, the first to the Chief

Constable of Berkshire, who had already been alerted by the Deputy Chief Constable and who was not only wide awake but had been on the point of telephoning Loftus himself; the second to Detective Chief Superintendent Knott, who was sleeping the sleep of the just in a small hotel outside Oxford, having that day brought to a successful conclusion the hunt for the killer of two Somerville students. One more jump forward in the rat race. A real possibility that he might make the coveted and difficult step up to Commander. It was a two-horse race really. Himself or Haliburton. And, as a result of the Oxford case, he fancied that his own nose was in front.

Success at Hannington could make a certainty of it. And success should not be too difficult. When a girl was killed you started with the 90 per cent probability that the killer was one of her boyfriends. In this case there was the extra possibility that it was a casual crime. The girl might have disturbed someone who was up to no good. A wild blow, not meant to kill. A panic-stricken flight. That would be much more difficult.

Could the missing window in the boathouse door be significant? How long ago had it been broken? He would have to ask Cavey about that. As the outlines of the investigation formed themselves in his mind, he began to consider what help he would need. He would have the two detective sergeants: McCourt and—what was the name?—think—Esdaile. McCourt had struck him as a cocky type who would be inclined to strike out a line on his own. He would want watching. For immediate purposes he would need more men. A lot more. The first step would be to contact Dennis Farr at Reading. He had met him in the course of the Oxford investigation and had got on well with him. Farr would help.

West Hannington merged into Hannington town. The change occurred quite suddenly. One moment he was in a village. The next moment in a suburb of small houses. Ten minutes more took him to the central point, where he turned left for the bridge over the river and the railway station and right up the main shopping street, near the far end of which was the police station.

Here he found Chief Inspector Dandridge waiting for him.

"Sorry to keep you up, Dan," he said. And if Dandridge was surprised that he should know, and use, his nickname he managed not to show it. "There's one or two things we've got to arrange before we all go to bed. First we've got to block both ends of the towpath. Trestles and a notice will do for the moment. One lot at Cavey's cottage, the other lot where River Park Avenue comes out. But notices won't keep the press out. We'll need a constable on duty at each end."

"I've only got—"

"Limited manpower. I know. That's the next thing. I'm going to give Farr a buzz and borrow a dozen men."

"A dozen?"

"For one day. Maybe two. After that we can rely on the men we've got here. With a little help from time to time. Next point: Who does your photography here?"

"That's Sergeant Esdaile."

"Christian name?"

"Everyone calls him Eddie."

"Is he O.K. with a camera? We don't want any slip-ups."

"He took a course at Roehampton."

"All right. Have him down there at first light. When he's done his stuff we can shift the body. We can probably arrange to have it taken straight down to Southampton for the autopsy. Not that I imagine they'll find out anything we didn't know already." He looked at some notes he had been scribbling on a scrap of paper. "Last point: Can you tell me where Dr. Farmiloe hangs out? I want a

48

word with him. Then we can all get a bit of shut-eye."

Dandridge gave him the address and directions for getting there. After Knott had gone he stood quite still for nearly a minute. In the same way that the recoil mechanism of a gun will nullify the shock of a shell's discharge, he seemed to be absorbing the impact of Detective Chief Superintendent Knott's personality.

As he went out through the charge room he looked at the clock over the Station Sergeant's desk and saw that it was exactly five o'clock. In an hour's time it would be fully light. He said goodnight to Sergeant Bakewell and went out into the street. He doubted whether he would get any sleep now, but he would go through the motions.

By nine o'clock Dandridge's office had quite a few people in it. Reading was represented by Chief Superintendent Oliphant of the Uniformed Branch and Detective Superintendent Farr of the C.I.D. McCourt and Esdaile were making themselves inconspicuous in the background. Shilling had set up a blackboard and was drawing a plan on it. Knott was standing beside the blackboard in a schoolmasterly attitude. Dr. Farmiloe was seated on the edge of the table with a sheaf of notes in one hand. Sergeant Bakewell had squeezed in and was effectively blocking the door. The window was wide open. It was going to be another scorching day.

"You've heard Dr. Farmiloe's report, gentlemen," said Knott. "It was extremely fortunate that he was able to be on the spot so quickly. And knew what he had to do when he got there."

A murmur of assent. All the senior officers present had suffered at one time or other the frustration of delayed or incompetent medical work.

"We shan't know for certain until we get the results of the autopsy, but it's fairly clear that Kate died at once, as the result of this single blow. Dr. Farmiloe has given us, as limits of the time of death, ten minutes to eleven and twenty minutes to twelve. He stressed that these were *outside* limits. A more probable time of death would be sometime between ten past and half past eleven."

He paused and then said, "It's a narrow time span. Geographically the area we have to consider is small, too."

He turned to the blackboard on which Shilling had finished his plan.

"We know that Kate left the Memorial Hall . . . there. At the point where Church Lane—Upper Church Lane, I think they call that bit—turns off and runs down to the river. Presumably she went straight down the lane. No evidence of that, but I can't see why she should have done anything different. The area on the left of the lane is Tennis Club property. All locked up. And there's a thick bramble hedge on the right. So let's assume that she made straight down the lane to the river."

"Distance?" said Oliphant.

Knott looked at Shilling, who said, "Two hundred yards, near enough."

"When she gets to the river she turns left, onto the towpath. That square at the corner is a cottage. It belongs to a bloke called Joe Cavey."

"The one who found the body?" said Farr.

"That's the man. The distance between his cottage and the boat shed is about twice the length of the lane, so call it four hundred yards. Say six hundred yards in all. It could have taken her around ten minutes to walk it."

"It was pitch dark," said Farr. "She couldn't have hurried. I'd say all of ten minutes, maybe a bit more."

"Agreed." Knott turned back to the plan. "There are no buildings between Cavey's corner and the boathouse. After the boathouse the path goes on again without buildings for about three hundred yards. It's not a large area. If we put enough men onto it we can comb it thoroughly."

"What are we looking for?" said Oliphant.

"Anything that's there," said Knott. The half smile that went with the words took some of the sting out of them. "But principally we're looking for a weapon. Something short and heavy, like an iron bar or a light axe. And here is where we've got to consider two different possibilities. Was it a planned killing, or was it just a hit-and-run job? If it was planned, we're not likely to find the weapon. There are too many places the killer could have hidden it. He could have buried it or thrown it into the river five miles away. On the other hand, if it was a panic job, the man will have slung the weapon away as quickly as possible. Into the bushes."

"More likely straight into the river," said Oliphant.

Knott helped himself to a piece of chalk and drew two lines across the Thames, one about fifty yards upstream from the boathouse and another a hundred yards downstream. He said, "I've laid on a team of divers from the Marine Commandos at Portsmouth. They're coming in later this morning. I've given them that piece of the river to search. If they don't find anything there, it'll be a waste of time to extend the search."

"You'll have to keep the pleasure boats away while that's going on," said Oliphant. "It won't be easy."

Farr agreed. He said, "If you stop the press boys coming down the towpath, first thing they'll do is hire boats and come down the river."

"I had thought about that," said Knott. "We can't keep people off the river altogether, but the Thames Conservancy have agreed to lend me one of their launches, with a crew and a loudspeaker. They'll see that no one gets too close. I'd like to borrow every man you can spare, Dennis. Make the search a saturation job. Get it finished in one day. Then we can lift most of the restrictions."

Oliphant said, "That certainly sounds a practical way of tackling it. Anyone got any comments?"

No one had any comments.

Knott said, "So much for search. When it comes to inquiry, we can take that a bit more deliberately. I'd like two experienced men from you, Dennis, to help Sergeant Esdaile and Sergeant McCourt in a house-to-house routine covering the area between Brickfield Road and the river." He was drawing further boundary lines on the board as he spoke. "I should guess that's about two hundred houses in all. Doing it carefully, we should be able to cover it in two or three days."

"Asking what in particular?" said Farr. "Apart from the obvious question of where people were between eleven and twelve last night, I mean."

"I'd be very interested in the movements of cars. If this was a planned job, the chances are the man came most of the way by car and did the last bit on foot."

Ian McCourt was aware that it was an occasion on which sergeants spoke little, or kept their mouths shut altogether. He ventured to say, "I think that almost all the people who knew Miss Steelstock well were at that dance at the Memorial Hall."

"The point had not escaped me," said Knott. "And the first job today for you and Esdaile will be to get round to everyone who was at the dance—and I mean everyone—and ask them to be present at eight o'clock tonight at the hall. If they ask why, tell them that they will be helping us to find out who killed Kate. If any of them won't cooperate, take their names and I'll talk to them later. And another thing. Tell them to come the same way they came last night. If it was by car, leave their cars in the same place."

"They'll all cooperate," said McCourt.

"All right. We've all got a lot to do. Anything else?"

"There's a crowd of men outside want to talk to you," said Sergeant Bakewell. "I think they're from the papers."

"I'll deal with them," said Knott.

As he stepped out into the High Street bulbs flashed and cameras clicked. Knott had arranged his face into a non-committal expression. Some years before, when he had been investigating a child murder, a photographer had taken a picture of him grinning. What he was laughing at was, in fact, a comment made by the local superintendent about the Chief Constable's wife. The paper, which was indulging in one of its anti-police crusades, had printed this picture alongside a picture of the small victim's mother in tears.

Knott said, "You'll understand, boys, that it's early days and I can't tell you anything much yet. I've always gone on the principle of working with the press, not against it. Anything I can tell you, I will. I'm staying at the Swan Inn, and if you care to come round at six o'clock this evening I'll see what I can do for you. One other thing. For today, you'll have to keep clear of that part of the towpath. We're planning to take it to pieces and put it together again. Right?"

"Any leads yet, Superintendent?"

"I've been on this job for six hours, son. If you care to say that I'm baffled, help yourself."

This produced the expected laugh. The reporters began to disperse. They recognized an old hand when they encountered one.

Knott caught Dandridge as he was leaving the station and said, "Somewhere I can have a quick word with you?"

"In my car. It's in the yard at the back."

He led the way around and they climbed in. Knott said, "This evening I'm going to meet a lot of the local characters. One thing I always like to find out first is, who are the nobs?"

Dandridge didn't pretend not to understand him. He said, "The biggest man round here, by a long chalk, is George Mariner. He's chairman of the local Bench, a District Councilor, president of the Boat Club and the Tennis Club and any other club you care to mention. Not only in Hannington. He's vice president of the Reading branch of the British Legion and patron of a boys' club in the East End of London."

"Married?"

"Wife, no children."

"Any particular reason?"

"Meet his wife."

Knott laughed and said, "Anyone else?"

"There's Group Captain Gonville, D.S.O., D.S.C. Retired now. A very nice chap. He's on the Bench, too. Our third J.P.'s a woman. Mrs. Havelock. She lives in a bungalow near the end of River Park Avenue, with a pack of tearaway kids."

Knott thought for a moment and said, "Shalimar or Heavealong?"

"Heavealong. You certainly seem to have picked up the local geography."

"I happened to notice them as I was walking back last night. That's one of only two places where you could get a car down onto the towpath. Who owns Shalimar?"

"Roseabel Tress. Artistic."

Knott grunted.

Well before eight o'clock that evening there was a sizable crowd outside the Memorial Hall. They watched the cars drive up, turn into the car park and station themselves carefully in their remembered places around one car that was still there, the cynosure of all eyes.

Katie's scarlet mini-Cooper.

Mr. Beaumorris, who had pedaled up on his ancient bicycle, said to Mrs. Havelock, "I feel like one of the minor guests at a royal wedding. A groom, or gardener, or some other humble functionary who has been invited and hides himself bashfully away behind the important guests." He did not look either bashful or humble. He looked rather pleased with himself.

Inside the hall the crowd tended to coalesce into the sort of groups they had formed on the previous evening. The chairs had been left undisturbed, and Mr. Beaumorris took possession of the one in the corner. Rosina Havelock and Harvey Maxton started to dance, but no one else thought this funny and they stopped at once when Mrs. Steelstock came in accompanied by Walter.

Eight o'clock struck from St. Michael's Church. The side door behind the stage opened and Detective Superintendent Knott stumped up the steps onto the stage and stationed himself in the center of it.

All eyes were on him. The silence was absolute.

SIX

Knott said in his gravelly voice, "I have been informed by the representatives of the press that what I am doing here tonight is reconstructing the crime. That's journalistic imagination. What I'm doing is quite different. I'm asking *you* to help *me.*"

There was a slight relaxing of tension. Was the man human after all?

"Most of you knew Katie and most of you, I guess, were very fond of her." His eye rested for a moment on Mrs. Steelstock sitting at the back of the hall. There was evidence of a sleepless night in her gray face and a livid smear under each eye, but her mouth was set in an uncompromising line.

"Our first job in a case like this is to establish times and places. Then we can do some elimination and get down to facts. It seemed to me that the quickest way of doing this was for all of you to write down—Sergeant Shilling here has got plenty of paper—as accurately as you possibly can, *when* you left the hall last night and *who* left with you and *where* you went. That's the reason I've got you all together. If one can't remember, the chances are someone else will be able to help him out. If you were in a party, discuss the matter. Someone will be sure to have looked at his watch. Someone will have said, 'We promised the baby sitter we'd be home by eleven,' or 'We wanted to get back to see the late night film on the box.' Talk about it. Argue about it. And when you've got the best answers you can, write your name and address on the top of the paper and give it back to the Sergeant. And let me assure you once more. There's no trick about this. All we're doing, in a manner of speaking, is to clear away the undergrowth. When that's done, we may be able to see a few of the trees."

As he said this he shifted his weight slightly, in a movement which seemed to throw his head forward. His eyes scanned the blur of faces in front of him. They were eyes which had seen a lot of brutality and stupidity and evasion and guilt.

"I believe he's trying to hypnotize us," said Mr. Beaumorris loudly to Mrs. Havelock. The audience was breaking up and re-forming into groups. A murmur of voices broke out and increased in volume. Suddenly everyone seemed to be talking at once.

"Like a cocktail party," said Georgie Vigors.

"A slow start," agreed Mr. Beaumorris, "but getting nicely under way with the second round of gins."

He had taken a fountain pen from his pocket and was staring at the sheet of paper which Sergeant Shilling had put into his hand.

"Not bad," said Knott as he shuffled through the papers. "Really not bad at all."

He was seated behind a big table in the room behind the courtyard at the back of Hannington police station. It had been cleared and equipped for him. The wall facing the window was papered with an overlay of map sheets of West Hannington. These were from the Land Registry Map Section at Tunbridge Wells and were on a scale of twenty-five inches to the mile, large enough to show individual houses and gardens. There was a smaller-scale map of the surrounding area, with the new M4 running like a yellow backbone down the middle of it, from Exit 12 south of Reading to Exit 13 on the Newbury–Oxford road.

"We've got three estimates of the time Kate left the hall. Young Vigors, who was dancing with her, says it was about eleven o'clock. He says she slipped away quietly, saying she didn't want to attract attention. Tony Windle confirms that. Another person who saw her go was Sally Nurse. She says it was a few minutes after eleven. Why she noticed the time was that she was surprised to see her go so early. Our Katie was usually one of the last to leave a party."

Shilling said, "That puts her at the boathouse between a quarter and twenty past eleven. Always supposing she went straight there. And that fits in well enough with the doctor's timings. He said most likely between ten past and half past eleven."

"Yes," said Knott. He thought about it, screwing up his eyes, as though he was looking into the sun. "It doesn't give them a lot of time for romance, does it?"

"Romance?"

"Kate and the chap she'd gone off to meet."

"How do you know she went to meet a chap?"

"When a girl cuts away from a dance on a warm summer night and goes down to a rendezvous on the riverbank, I'd be surprised if she'd gone to meet her stockbroker and talk about investments. Maybe that's because I've got a dirty mind."

Shilling, who had been turning over duplicate copies of the papers on his desk, said, "If you're right, it cuts out almost everyone who was at the dance."

"That's what I was thinking," said Knott. "What we've got is a lot of nice interlocking stories. Here's the score to date. The Mariners left, by car, just after Kate. Mr. and Mrs. Nurse a few minutes later. Then that old pansy. What's his name?"

"Beaumorris."

"Right. Frank Beaumorris. Used to work in the manuscript department at the Victoria and Albert."

Shilling looked up for a moment and said, "Did you run into him by any chance?"

"I did," said Knott. He seemed disinclined to pursue the subject. "He pedaled off at around ten past eleven. Old Vigors went off by car shortly after that. He put it at a quarter past. Then we've got a foursome, the Gonvilles and the parson and his wife. They went together to the Gonvilles' house for a cup of coffee and stayed there nattering until around midnight. Mrs. Steelstock and her son, that po-faced boy—name?"

"Walter," said Shilling. He had a list of names in front of him and seemed to have been memorizing them. "Works in an insurance office in Reading."

"Right. They were away by eleven twenty. The last to go was the big woman—"

"Mrs. Havelock. J.P. Seven children. Three of them at the dance."

"She took her three kids with her. And that dotty character—wait for it—Tress. Roseabel Tress. Lives next door to her in a bungalow called 'Shalimar.' If anyone came that way, she'll have heard them. A real nosey old virgin."

"If you take the latest possible time of death, eleven forty," said Shilling, "it's *just* possible, I suppose, for any of those people to have driven their cars to the end of River Park Avenue, walked along the towpath and been in time to kill Kate."

"It's possible," said Knott. "But I don't believe it. I don't think anyone who was at the dance killed her. I think they're all as innocent as they sound. No. Someone was there waiting for her. Someone who'd planned to get her to just that spot and meant to kill her."

Shilling had worked with Knott on a number of cases. It had not taken him long to realize that the Superintendent was not an intellectual man, was not, in most senses of the word, clever. But he had one faculty which was based partly on shrewdness and partly on experience. He could grasp the shape and outline of any crime he was called on to investigate. He could sense whether it was a professional job or an amateur job, whether it was motivated by greed or fright or frustration, whether it was the outcome of careful premeditation or thoughtless fury. It was an instinct which had very rarely let him down and had brought him to the eminence he enjoyed.

"I can tell you something else, too," he said. "You can forget about passing tramps or interrupted burglars. When I said that, I hadn't seen her bag. That spells premeditation. No question."

The bag had been found by the searchers. It was an

evening dress bag, a pretty little thing with a pattern of roses woven in silk on the outside. The contents were laid out on the table beside it: a running-repair kit, a double folder of oiled silk with a sponge in one pocket and a box in the other labeled "Toasty Beige"; a cylinder labeled "Pearl Spin Eye Glaze"; a lipstick labeled "Mulberry"; a couple of tissues; and a folded pound note.

"If she'd been knocked on the head by some toe-rag who happened to be passing, first he'd have been too scared to stop and search her bag. Second, if he *had* searched it, he'd have taken the money."

"Someone did search it," said Shilling.

There was a photograph of the bag lying where it had been found in the long grass a few feet from the body. The contents were scattered beside it and the silk lining had been ripped half out.

"Right," said Knott. "Someone opened it in a hurry and took something out of it. And I guess we know what he took, don't we?"

Shilling smiled and said, "No marks for guessing. He was looking for the note he'd sent her, asking her to meet him at the boathouse."

"That's for sure."

"And if there was a note in the bag," said Shilling, smiling in the shy way that made him look a lot younger and more defenseless than he really was, "it wasn't the only thing the killer took. Where are her car keys?"

Knott shot a sharp look at his assistant and then said, "Full marks for that one, Bob. I'd missed it. Do you think they could have fallen out somewhere?"

"If they had, I guess the searchers would have found them. They didn't miss much."

The search of the previous day had produced a mass of curious articles. The obvious rubbish and anything at all old or rusty had been put in a basket under the table. On

60

the table were spread the more promising finds. They included a scout's knife, a small compass of the type used by escaping prisoners of war, three twelve-bore shotgun cartridges, an old-fashioned collar stud, a new type tenpenny piece, an old type half crown and a torn shred of gray flannel.

Knott said, "That came off the barbed wire in the field next to Cavey's cottage. And from what he told us, I can make a good guess where it came from."

Shilling was still looking at the contents of the evening dress bag. He said, "I suppose all these things have been dusted." When Knott nodded he picked up the cylinder labeled "Eye Glaze" and drew a line on the back of his hand. Then he repeated the process with the lipstick and regarded the result critically.

He said, "Not such a terribly with-it girl, our Kate."

"What do you mean?"

"They're top-class stuff all right. But blue eye shadow rather went out last year. The fashionable shade this year is blue-brown. It's called "Livid." And I don't think a blonde who was really giving her mind to it would have used mulberry lipstick. Much more suitable for a brunette."

"I can see you haven't been wasting your evenings off," said Knott. "Maybe it was all part of the pose. The simple village girl sporting with the yokels. We don't really know much about her yet."

He paused for a long moment, standing hunched and still in front of the side table, looking down at the odd collection of exhibits but not seeing them. His mind was moving over the information he had collected; over the statements and the photographs and the impressions he had gathered while talking to people. Already he could see the killer. He was standing in the shadow of the boathouse waiting for the girl he had summoned, the girl who must have thought he was in love with her, or at least harmless, or she would not have come tripping so boldly down that dark path to meet him.

He said, "There's one mistake we mustn't make. She didn't spend all her time down here. She had two lives. One of them was lived up in London. We'll have to divide this. Get back to London first thing on Monday and see her agent. I've got his name and address here somewhere." He searched through a bulging wallet and extracted a card. "Mark Holbeck, 22a Henrietta Street, Covent Garden. He'll know as much as anyone about her. Don't be too long about it. I'll want you back down here. I've a feeling we should be able to clear this one up pretty quickly."

He picked up the internal telephone and said, "Eddie? Would you and Ian come in for a moment, please." He used their Christian names with a slight hint of irony, as if it was all part of man management and he knew it and they knew it. To Metropolitan officers, country policemen were Swedes. Men who checked the rear lights on bicycles, dealt with sheep-chasing dogs and could recognize a Colorado beetle when they saw one, but knew nothing about the realities of serious crime.

"One of them took some nice photographs," said Shilling. "That must have been Eddie."

They were good clear color prints, taken from directly over the object so as not to distort its dimensions, with a yard rule lying alongside each. They showed the body of Kate as it lay face down clasping mother earth. There was a close-up of the deep fractured wound in her head above the right ear, as though someone had been standing directly behind her and she had half turned her head, perhaps sensing at the last moment that there was someone there.

"Right," said Knott. "Here's how we split it up. Ian, you tackle the Havelocks and the Tress woman. Eddie, you take the Nurses. The one I'm interested in is the girl, Sally. She seems to have gone for a midnight spin with young Gonville. Interesting to compare their stories. That's why I want them taken separately. Then you can have a word with the parson and the Group Captain and their trouble-and-strifes."

Esdaile said, "Is there anything in particular you want us to find out? I mean, they all seem to be—"

"They're all as white as driven snow," said Knott. "What I'm interested in is two things in particular. Whether they saw, or heard, anyone else on the move around that time. And what they knew or thought about Katie. What sort of girl she was. What her interests were. Who were her special friends. They may be a bit shy of talking about that, but if you go about it the right way you'll probably get there in the end. All those people should be available, being Sunday." He paused, then added, "There's one other thing. Don't rely on your memories. Take these with you. They'll save you a lot of trouble afterwards."

He pushed toward each of them a contraption the size of a small camera. "Put it in your side pocket. It will pick up a voice speaking normally at five paces. Don't forget to switch it on."

Esdaile had picked up the box and was fingering it lovingly. He was a man with a passion for mechanical devices. He said, "That's a great little machine."

McCourt said, "I take it that these tape recordings will be in place of written statements."

"Wrong," said Knott. "I want both. I want the tape *and* your transcription of it. And I want them both by six o'-clock every evening."

"The thoughts of all of us present here today," said the Reverend Bird, "must be focused on the tragedy which has struck our happy community like a bolt from the blue. It would be idle to pretend otherwise. It is in times like this that we have to ask ourselves reverently, but seriously, why God should permit such things to happen."

Matins at eleven o'clock was the popular service in West Hannington. It allowed the men to get to the club for their pre-lunch drink and the women time to cook the lunch for which the men were going to be late coming back from their pre-lunch drink. On this occasion St. Michael's Church was unusually full.

("It's the cohesive effect of shock," Mr. Beaumorris had explained to Georgie Vigors when he met her in the porch. "How it does bring people together!")

"Katie was not our private possession. She belonged to the whole country. Nevertheless, having been born here and living here, she had a very special place in our hearts."

There was a stir at the back of the church, as of an animal moving.

"In spite of her public fame we all knew her for a simple, natural, lovable girl—"

"Stop it," said a loud and angry voice. "Stop it at once. Leave Katie alone. Get on with your preaching."

All heads jerked around. The rector seemed to be paralyzed by the interruption.

Jonathan Limbery was on his feet. His face was scarlet. "You none of you knew anything about her. And now she's dead, so for God's sake let her lie."

The two churchwardens, George Mariner and Group Captain Gonville, were moving down the aisle toward him.

Their advance seemed to provoke Jonathan. His voice rose to a cracked shout. "All right, you pious hypocrites. You can throw me out, but it's not going to stop me telling the truth."

"Come along, old man."

"She was a bitch."

"Take his other arm, Gerry. You can't make scenes like this in church."

"Leave me alone. I'm going. I wouldn't want to stay here and listen to a lot of drip like that."

Jonathan stalked to the door, shepherded by the church-wardens. When he reached it he swung around as though to say something else, but the Group Captain pushed him kindly but decisively through the door and followed him out. He said to Mariner, "I'll look after him, George. You get back and stand by the rector. I thought he was going to pass out."

Mariner went back into the now completely silent church. The rector was standing motionless in the pulpit gripping the rail in front of him, his face white. Mariner plodded back to his seat, his footsteps sounding loudly on the tiles of the floor. As he reached the pew the rector came to life. He said in a loud clear voice, "And now to God the Father, God the Son and God the Holy Ghost we ascribe as is most justly due all might, majesty, dominion and power, now, henceforth and for ever more." The liturgy of the Church of England swung back onto its course.

It was during the singing of the last hymn that the Group Captain returned and made his way back to his seat. In response to the raised eyebrow of his wife he mouthed at her, "Gone home."

"Well," said Mr. Beaumorris to Mrs. Havelock, "what are we supposed to make of that?"

"Nothing we didn't know already. Limbery is un-balanced. Some regulator inside him isn't working."

"Whatever he may have thought about Katie's character and—um—disposition, church was hardly the appropriate place to voice it."

"It wasn't very tactful."

"Although actually, strictly between you and me and with all deference to the feeling about *nil nisi bonum de mortuis,* it has to be admitted that there were times when our Katie did behave rather bitchily."

"Isn't it a crime, or a felony, or something?" said Mariner.

"Sacrilege? Yes. It's still on the statute book," said Vernon Vigors. "It's usually breaking into churches and smashing or defiling the sacred ornaments, something like that. There were those ultra Protestants who used to smash up altars."

"You don't think that interrupting the sermon comes into the same category?"

"It's a moot point," said Vigors.

SEVEN

When Knott had asked Ian McCourt if he knew how to take a plaster cast, McCourt had said nothing but had simply nodded. One reason for this was that he was beginning to find Knott's manner irritating and he felt that the less he said to him the better. The other reason was that he thought he did, in fact, know how to set about it.

The reason for his confidence was that he had recently read in an old copy of the *Police Journal* an article entitled "Traces of Footwear, Tires and Tools" by Detective Constable Douglas Hamilton of the City of Glasgow Police.

He had the journal with him as he pored over the faint marks in the sandy patch between the end of Roseabel Tress's garden and the first of the building plots. A car had been driven a few yards up the towpath and then backed onto this patch, but not very far. The prints had been made by a small portion of both rear tires, rather more by the off side than the near.

"An impression in moist firm earth can be reproduced without any preliminary treatment. But when impressions are found in loose earth or sand it is advisable to 'fix' the surface before pouring in the plaster, since without this the weight of the plaster will distort the formation of the loose surface."

McCourt looked at the sand. It was totally dry and friable. The sharp edges of the tire marks had already started to smooth out. Clearly they would have to be "fixed." What did Detective Constable Hamilton say about that?

"A solution of shellac in methylated spirits or a cellulose acetate solution may be used with excellent results. A very light coating only should be applied."

Fine, thought McCourt. No doubt the Glasgow central police station was equipped with shellac, methylated spirits and acetate solution. But how was he supposed to find them in Hannington on a Sunday?

A shadow fell across the sand.

"Something troubling you, son?" said Knott.

McCourt scrambled to his feet. Knott stooped down and picked up the journal which had been open on the ground beside him. He studied it for a long moment and then said, "You ought to keep up to date in the techniques of your profession. You're not married, are you?"

"No."

"Got a girlfriend?"

"Well—"

67

"Or a mother or an aunt or a landlady. Someone who'll lend you a hairspray?"

"Every now and then," said Roseabel Tress, "I do take a little sleeping pill. It's not my regular habit, you understand. They're fairly mild, not what you'd describe as knockout drops. Helen Mariner put me onto them. She gets them from her doctor. So you see, I shouldn't be a very effective witness. But it's true, yes. I did hear a car."

"About what time might that have been?" said McCourt.

"Let me think. We got away from the dance before half past eleven and came straight back here in Constantia Havelock's car. She asked me in for a cup of tea. Then there was that business about Roney and Sim—"

"I heard about that."

"I don't suppose I was more than twenty minutes in their house. When I got back I went straight to bed."

"Then it would have been soon after midnight when you heard the car."

"That's right. Five or ten minutes after."

"Was it coming, or going?"

"Oh, going. I'm sure of that. It would have been parked on the path, I imagine. I heard it start up. And I heard it drive off, down the avenue. I—yes, that's right. I heard it drive away."

McCourt's ear picked up the change of tone in her voice, the note of panic, and looking down saw that her hands, which had been lying loosely in her lap, were now clasped so tightly that her knuckles were white and the bones at the back were standing out.

He said, "What is it, Miss Tress? Is something wrong?"

'Nothing," she said. "It's nothing. I'm sorry. I was stupid   Her self-possession was coming back slowly. "I just remembered something. It was rather unpleasant. I hardly know how to explain it."

"Try."

"It was just that . . . well, the fact is that I'm a seventh child of seven. All my life I've known that I have these powers. I read a most interesting article about them the other day. I understand that they are now known as extra-sensory perception. There's quite a scientific basis for them."

The word "scientific" seemed to reassure her. She looked at McCourt to see how he was taking it. He smiled and said, "Science is explaining a lot of things we used to call miraculous. What exactly was it that you felt when you haird the car driving away?"

"Evil, Sergeant. Naked evil."

"Yes, I heard it go," said Mrs. Havelock, "a little after midnight. That would be right."

"Could you tell from the noise it made what sort of car it was?"

"I'm afraid all cars sound the same to me. If one of the boys had heard it, they'd probably be able to tell you. But they sleep at the back."

McCourt opened his briefcase and produced a torn scrap of gray flannel. He said, "This was found on the barbed wire of the field by Cavey's cottage."

"And I can tell you *exactly* where it came from," said Mrs. Havelock. She opened her sewing basket and produced a pair of boy's flannel shorts. "You can match it up if you like."

"Aye, that's where it came from, no doubt," said McCourt. "Which of them was it?"

"Sim. He's the nine-year-old. Roney's eleven. They're as bad as each other. Beyond parental control, Sergeant. They need a father's hand."

"I'll have a word with them in a moment. There are just the one or two things I'd like to clear up first. You all drove home between twenty and half past eleven?"

"About then."

"Which way did you come?"

"Straight down the street and turned right into the avenue."

"Did you pass anyone?"

"No one at all. I'm pretty sure of that. You could ask Roseabel Tress."

"I have," said McCourt. "She agrees with you. She doesn't remember passing anyone. Tell me, Mrs. Havelock, what did you think of Katie?"

"That's a fast ball."

"A fast ball?" said McCourt, with the hesitation of someone who had been educated in a school which regarded cricket as a game played by southerners to fill in the awkward gap between two football seasons. "You mean it was an unfair question? I'm sorry."

"Not unfair. Unexpected. What *did* I think about her? It's a difficult question. She was two quite different people, of course. When she was here she liked to play the simple home-loving girl who went out with the boy next door—or one of the two or three boys next door—lived with Mum and went to church on Sundays."

"You said 'play'?"

"Oh, I think so. After all, that was the character she put over in her television appearances. She can't really have been as simple as that. If she had been, she'd never have got where she did. I don't know what goes on behind the scenes in television, but I should imagine it's one of the toughest rat races there are. And working in London's not the same as working down here."

"When I was in London," said McCourt, "everything seemed to go twice as fast and sound twice as loud as it does in the country. I'd like to have a word with the boys."

"With me here?"

"Certainly. I don't want to frighten them."

"I sometimes wish," said Mrs. Havelock, "that I'd found some way of doing it."

Roney and Sim were waiting outside the door. They bounded in looking excited and important but not at all apprehensive.

"Well, now," said McCourt, "what were you up to on Friday night?"

Roney told him. McCourt had found that boys usually made good witnesses. They stuck to the facts. He said, "This question of timing is becoming rather important. When exactly did you leave the dance?"

"When we saw Mum driving off. That's why we ran. We wanted to get back ahead of her. We might have done, only old Cavey shouted at us and Sim got caught up in that barbed wire. After that we went more slowly."

"In that case," said McCourt, "you must have been walking down the towpath at around twenty-five to twelve."

"That's right," said Roney. He shot a look at Sim, who was bouncing gently up and down on the edge of his chair, looking like a kettle coming to the boil. He opened his mouth to say something but Roney cut him off with the firmness of two years' seniority. He said, "From what we read in the papers, she must have been dead by then, wouldn't you say?"

In his Saturday evening briefing, Knott had given out the presumed time of death. It had been done quite deliberately, weighing advantage against disadvantage.

"It seems possible," said McCourt cautiously.

"Then," said Roney, "she must have been lying there on the grass when we went past."

Sim could contain himself no longer. He said, "We might have met the murderer coming away."

The two boys looked at each other with an equal mixture of horror and excitement.

71

"It's lucky you didn't," said McCourt.

When he had gone Mrs. Havelock said, "What are you two keeping back?"

"We're not keeping anything back, are we, Sim?"

Sim said, "No. Honestly we're not, Mum."

Mrs. Havelock looked at her sons. She was thinking, In about two years' time I shall have to start treating Roney as though he was grown up. It wasn't too bad with Michael. He was pretty reasonable. Roney's different.

The two boys stared solemnly back at her. In the end she said, "If there *is* anything else, it must be told. This isn't a game."

"I can't tell you a great deal," said Tony Windle, "because I was almost the last away from the hall. Old Cavey came in looking like death and started clearing people out and I asked him what was bothering him and . . . well . . . he told me."

"Can you remember what he said?"

"Not the exact words. But I do remember I was surprised."

"Why?"

Tony thought about it. Then he said, "He didn't wrap it up at all. It was something like 'She's dead. Someone smashed her head in.' As if he was talking about someone he didn't really know."

"But he did know her?"

"Of course he knew her. Everyone knew Katie. He'd taught her to punt when she was eight and picked her out of the river when she fell in."

"And everyone loved her."

"Is that a question," said Tony coolly, "or a statement?"

"I suppose it was a sort of question."

"When she was a little girl with a snub nose and pigtails, certainly everyone loved her. Everyone loves little girls.

When she grew up, naturally things got a bit more compli-
cated. Either you loved her, or you liked her, or you didn't
care one way or the other."

"And which category did you fall into?"

"Something between two and three. I think we both regarded each other, in a different sort of way, as an asset.
If I took Katie to a function, I could be sure that everyone
else there was envying me. That was the plus as far as I
was concerned. From her point of view, I was a useful
attendant-cum-door-opener-cum-chauffeur. With a kiss
last thing instead of a tip."

"And nothing more?"

"I regret to say, Sergeant, nothing more. Just a conve-
nience. Give you an example. I'd have been expected to
pick her up in my car and take her to that dance on Friday
night. Despite the fact that she was within walking distance of the hall, and if she hadn't wanted to walk, her own
car was parked in the stableyard outside her flat. But it
would have been a bore to have got in and started up the
engine. Much better to rely on good old Tony."

"But she *did* take her own car."

"Only because mine was out of action, being minus its
distributor head. And there wasn't really much time to ask
anyone else."

"You're making her out to be rather a heartless sort of
girl."

"All girls are heartless," said Tony, with the ac-
cumulated wisdom of twenty-five years. Then he corrected
himself. "Heartless is the wrong word. Katie had a heart
buried deep down. Given the right sort of man, she'd have
gone overboard like any other girl. I wasn't the right type,
that was all."

"And what do you think would have been the right
type?"

"You're fishing."

73

"Aye," said McCourt placidly. "I'm fishing."

Tony thought about this and then said, "All right. I'm only telling you what anyone else who knew her would tell you. She wanted two different things. From a man she wanted passion. She wanted someone who could really let himself go. And out-and-outer. But even while she was letting herself go, the dispassionate part of her would have been saying, 'I wonder whether he couldn't be some use to me, do something for me, help me in my career.'"

"How can you be sure of that?"

"I'm sure of it," said Tony, "because on one occasion she actually told me so. I remember it, because normally she didn't talk about herself. I think she'd had one drink above her ration; which was unusual, too, because she kept as firm an eye on her drink intake as she did on every other aspect of her life."

Tony seemed to have lost track of what he had started to say. McCourt prodded him gently back. He said, "And what was it she told you?"

"Oh, we'd had a bit of a quarrel. I think I started it by implying that she relied too much on my services and if she wasn't a bit nicer to me I might think twice about doing things for her and so on. That annoyed her. She said, 'The trouble with you, Tony, is that you don't amount to anything and never will. The most you'll ever end up as is "something in insurance." That's no good to a girl like me. What I need is people with influence. People who can help me out when I get into trouble. I've got friends like that up in London. And I've got at least one *very* useful friend down here.' I asked her who it was and she wouldn't tell me. I pulled her leg about it when we next met up. I asked her who Mr. Big was. She denied having said anything about it. I think she was sorry she'd opened her mouth. And I think I'm talking too much."

"On the contrary," said McCourt, "you've been most

74

helpful. One other question. When you got home, did you go straight to bed?"

"Actually, no. It was too bloody hot. I sat up and waited for Billy. I wanted to find out what he'd been up to."

"With Sally Nurse?"

"Yes. It didn't seem to amount to much. We had a bit of a natter and split a bottle of beer out of the fridge. It must have been half past one, or even later, before we finally went up. Oh, and I remember we heard Jonathan coming back. He'd been out on some job for the paper. A fire or something, wasn't it?"

"I believe it was," said McCourt.

"Everyone seems to think," said Billy Gonville, "that if you take a girl out for a midnight spin in your car your intentions are dishonorable."

"And they're wrong, of course."

"Not necessarily. What they're overlooking is that your intentions are unimportant. It's the girl's intentions that matter. With some girls you don't have to think twice. They've started undressing before you've got the car into second gear."

"But with Miss Nurse it was different?"

"Sally's a nice girl. A very nice girl." McCourt wasn't certain whether admiration or regret was the predominant note in young Mr. Gonville's voice. "The trouble is, she's been too much under Katie's shadow. Following her round, imitating her getup, all that sort of thing. She'd buried her own personality. I thought it was time it was unburied."

"Then you regarded this midnight run as a sort of therapy?"

Billy looked at him suspiciously and said, "Look here, Sergeant, you're meant to be inquiring into a crime. Not exploring my sex life."

"I'm sorry," said McCourt. He always found it difficult to maintain an official attitude with Windle and Gonville. They were all much of an age. Off duty, they used each other's Christian names without embarrassment. "Could you tell me where you went?"

"No difficulty. We started along the by-road, took the A329 as far as Streatley and then went straight on, until we hit the north–south road between Newbury and Oxford. Went down it a few miles to that junction with the M4."

"That's Access Point Thirteen."

"Right. Up to then we'd had to take it easy. Still a lot of traffic about. When we got onto the motorway I let her rip. We must have damn near made a ton."

"Please remember I'm a policeman."

"So you are. I'd forgotten. Anyway, luckily I'd eased off a bit when we were stopped."

"You were stopped?"

"At Access Fourteen, south of Reading. The police had the road blocked. A lot of cars queuing up. Took everyone's names and addresses. Surely you know about it. They had a ring round the whole area. Trying to catch the people who did Yattendon House."

"I haird something about it; we weren't directly involved. I gather they didn't catch anyone."

"Total flop. They kept it up until three in the morning and netted one or two men out with other people's wives. The burglars were too smart for them."

"After Access Fourteen?"

"We went home. I had Sally back at her house about one fifteen. Both parents still up. Rather a frosty reception."

"So I should imagine," said McCourt. "Could you be a bit more definite about some of those times?"

"Let's think." Billy Gonville pressed his lips together and wrinkled his brow to demonstrate thought. "When we were all asked by Superintendent Dracula to write down our times, I had a word with various other girls I'd been dancing with and the general opinion seemed to be that we cleared out around ten forty-five."

"And up to that point you'd been dancing continuously?"

"Non-stop. I can't tell you all the girls' names because some I didn't know. A pity we didn't have those old-fashioned dance cards. Anyway, if you asked anyone living in Lower Church Lane they'd have been bound to have heard me. Coming and going."

McCourt was inclined to agree. Gonville had modified the fishtail exhaust on his Austin-Healey Sprite so that it now boomed like a bittern. He said, "Going at a reasonable pace"—he was studying the local ordnance sheet which he had brought with him—"it took you how long to get to Access Thirteen? I make it about fifteen miles."

"All right. Say thirty minutes."

"And from there to Access Fourteen?"

"No time at all. When you give that car her head she practically takes off. You can see why they call her a sprite."

"All right. Ten minutes. That gets you to Fourteen at twenty-five past twelve."

"We were held up there answering questions for five minutes."

"But," said McCourt, "if you left there at half past twelve, how did it take you three-quarters of an hour to get home?"

"We stopped for a bit. For a talk."

"For a talk?"

"For a talk," said Gonville firmly. "I told you I thought she needed bringing out." He started to laugh. "She's an odd kid. Do you know what her real ambition is? She wants to be adopted."

"By anyone in particular?"

"No. Just by someone. She feels she's picked the wrong parents."

Roney and Sim were squatting among a pile of deck chairs and punt cushions at the short end of the L-shaped balcony which screened the front and side of their bungalow. It was their favorite place for private discussions, and this discussion was both private and important.

Sim said, "Don't you think we ought to tell someone?"

"No," said Roney. He said it quickly but firmly, as though he'd been thinking about it a lot and had come to an irrevocable decision.

"Well, I don't know," said Sim.

"You promised."

"I know I promised, but—"

"There aren't any buts about it. You promised, and if you don't keep your word I'll . . . I'll skin you alive."

They were sitting so close together that their noses were nearly touching. Sim said very seriously, "You know what Mum said. This isn't a game. It's murder."

"Why should it have anything to do with murder?"

"Well, Johnno used to meet her there. More than once. *We* know that."

"All right. He used to meet her there. Just because people meet each other it doesn't mean they kill each other, does it?"

"I suppose not," said Sim unhappily.

"Then promise you're not going to say anything about it."

"I've promised already."

"Promise again."

"Well, *I* think he ought to tell the police," said Rosina. She had been standing out of sight around the corner, listening.

The two boys scrambled up. Roney was bright red in the

face. He said, "Sneak, sneak, sneak. You've been listening."

"Certainly I've been listening. And lucky I was listening, because otherwise I suppose nobody would ever have heard about this."

Roney took a step toward his sister. He was almost as tall as she was. He said in a voice which was rising out of restraint, "You filthy little cow. Sneaking round. Listening. If you say a word to anyone I'll kill you."

"Don't be daft."

"If you don't promise, I'll kill you."

"Of course I'm not going to promise—"

Roney jumped at her, his hands groping for her face. He was sobbing with fury. Rosina gave a cry as his nails scored her cheek. Sim said weakly, "Roney, don't. Don't."

And at that moment Mrs. Havelock appeared in the doorway. She said, "Leave Rosina alone."

"I'm going to kill her," said Roney. He had hold of her hair with one hand and was scrabbling at her face with the other. Mrs. Havelock took one step forward and hit him. She was a big, strong woman. The blow knocked him down and knocked most of the breath and all the fight out of him. Sim was crying. Rosina was mopping the scratch on her cheek with a handkerchief.

Disregarding Roney, Mrs. Havelock said, "Will one of you now tell me what all that was about?"

Rosina said, "I heard them talking. About the boathouse." She hesitated for a moment, as if conscious of what she was going to do.

"Well?"

"They knew that Jonathan used to meet Katie there at night. They used to creep along and spy on them. Just like they did on Lavinia in the churchyard. Beasts."

Mrs. Havelock said, "Is that true?"

Sim gulped out, "Yes. I knew we ought to say. Roney made me promise."

"Why on earth did you do that, Roney?"

Roney said nothing.

"I expect he was in love with Jonathan," said Rosina spitefully.

EIGHT

The Boat Club and the Tennis Club shared a bar which was part of the Tennis Club pavilion. This was a convenient arrangement, since most people belonged to both clubs.

On that Sunday morning it was crowded and Mr. Cavey was busier than usual serving gins and tonics with ice and pints of warm beer.

"We have carried out our religious duty," said Mr. Beaumorris to his confidante, Georgie Vigors, "by going to church and vowing to love our neighbor as ourselves. We can now perform our social duty by dissecting our neighbor's character."

"If you're talking about Jonathan," said Georgie, "I can't say I was entirely surprised. He's been working up for an explosion for months. Actually, I had a certain amount of sympathy for him. I think Dickybird could have left Kate out of his sermon."

"Oughtn't you to be sitting down?" said her husband.

"Hullo, hullo," said Mr. Beaumorris, "are you pregnant, woman?"

"It's on the cards. Noel's in the fussing stage. I'm told it lasts for quite a week."

"Husbands suffer terribly over their first child," said Mavis Gonville. "I thought Gerry was going to pass out when I told him. He had to be revived with a large brandy."

"I've never touched brandy since," said the Group Captain. "It would bring back memories. Have you had a visitation yet?"

Noel Vigors looked blank. Gonville said, "The buzz is that the fuzz—I say, that's rather good. Buzz-fuzz. Fuzz-buzz."

"Get on with it."

"Well, they're said to be going round to everyone who was at the dance asking a lot of questions. Sergeant McCourt was in Riverside Avenue grilling Roseabel Tress and the Havelocks."

"As long as it's just McCourt or Esdaile," said Mavis. "That little white Superintendent gives me the creeps."

"He's a dangerous man," said Mr. Beaumorris. "As I have every reason to know." He had raised his voice sufficiently to receive the attention of everyone near him.

"Come on, Frank."

"Tell us the worst. What episode in your murky past did he have to investigate?"

"It wasn't my past," said Mr. Beaumorris. "It was when I was at the V. and A. It was some years ago. Knott wasn't on the Murder Squad. He was a detective inspector at the local station. The auditors had unearthed a rather serious discrepancy in the imprest account of the Far Eastern Section. One of the cashiers was suspected. An old man called Connington. Bill Connington. Knott really took him to pieces. He was grilling him for most of the day and part of the evening."

Mr. Beaumorris picked up his glass of shandy and

finished it while his audience waited. Then he got to his feet and picked up his walking stick.

"Really, Frank," said old Mr. Vigors. "You can't leave us all in suspense. What happened? Was Connington guilty?"

"It was never *completely* established. He cut his throat that same night. With an antique Malayan kris." He pottered to the door. "My young lady will have my luncheon ready. She gets very cross if I'm late."

Mavis said, "I sometimes wonder if Frank isn't the biggest old humbug in the whole village. *Could* you cut your throat with a kris?"

"You can cut your throat with anything if you give your mind to it," said her husband. "I remember one young pilot officer—"

"Not before lunch," said Georgie Vigors firmly. "And who is Frank's young lady? I didn't know he had one."

"It's a girl called Myra," said Mavis. "Don't know her surname. Her sister's Polly. The one who does for the Mariners."

"So *that's* where he gets all his gossip from," said Georgie.

It was Polly who opened the front door of the Croft to Superintendent Knott. She was back on her Jeeves impersonation and paced in front of him to the study. Mariner, who had a sense of protocol, kept him waiting for only two minutes. This compared with the five he would have allotted to Inspector Dandridge and anything up to twenty for Sergeant McCourt, whom he disliked as much as the Sergeant disliked him.

"I can't tell you much more than I put down on that paper," he said. "My wife and I left at about eleven o'clock. A lot of people seem to have seen us go. My wife doesn't like to be up late. She sleeps badly. She went to bed immediately we got home."

"That young personage who let me in. Does she live here?"

"Polly? No. You can't get residential staff nowadays. Not in West Hannington anyway."

"Difficult enough in London," agreed the Superintendent.

"She's willing, under protest, to stop in while we're out at night. In return for suitable reimbursement. She was sitting in for us on Friday night."

"But she took off as soon as you got back?"

"As soon as she heard our car in the drive. The young haven't much sense of duty these days."

"They like to live their own lives," said Knott. The making of trite remarks like this enabled him to divorce his mind from the conversation and devote it to taking in impressions. Impressions of his surroundings, of the man he was talking to, of tension or relaxation. Mariner seemed to be easy enough. A cock on his own dunghill.

"So what did you do then?"

Mariner looked surprised and said, "Well, I didn't go to bed at once. I had a whisky and soda. In here, actually. Which reminds me—"

"Not at the moment, thank you."

"I finished reading the local papers. Put out the dog. Locked up the house. I expect it would have been midnight before I went up."

"I imagine that one of your reasons for hanging about would be to allow your wife to get off to sleep?"

"Actually we sleep in different rooms."

Knott said, so casually that the thought might only just have occurred to him, "I meant to ask you. What did you think of Kate? You knew her quite well, I imagine."

"Not particularly well." Mariner thought about it. "She was a nice unspoiled kid. When she made such a success of her television career, it might have turned her head.

Perhaps it did, a little. But not nearly as much as you might have expected. Mind you, we only saw the Hannington side of her."

"And the outside of the London side."

"I don't follow you."

"The side that came over on the television screen."

"Oh yes. Well, my wife and I aren't great television watchers."

"But you have a set," Knott said with a smile. "The great detective demonstrates his methods. I saw the aerial."

Mariner said, "Yes, we have a set. It's kept in the kitchen. We have it brought in here if there's something we particularly want to watch. Wimbledon or a test match."

"I imagine she didn't lack for admirers," said Knott. He had often found this simple technique surprisingly useful. Let the conversation drift, then pull it back with a jerk. On this occasion the result was surprising. Mariner flushed, started to say something, changed his mind and then grunted out, "Of course she had. Dozens of them. Round her like flies."

"Anyone in particular?"

Mariner was recovering himself. He said in a more normal voice, "Her accepted squire was young Tony Windle, but I don't think he meant anything more to her than a free taxi service."

"But there's someone else?"

"There *was* someone else. Until about a month ago. The general impression was that the only serious proposition was Jonathan Limbery."

"And what happened to Jonathan?"

"Katie and he had a flaming row. In public. In the Tennis Club bar."

"I'd like to hear about that."

Mariner thought about it. Knott was watching his face. He said to himself, Even if I hadn't asked him, he was going to tell me about it. There's some sort of personal involvement here. Either he dislikes Limbery, or maybe he was after the girl himself. You can never tell with these middle-aged men.

Mariner said, "It was early in the evening. There were only five of us there. Kate and her brother Walter. They'd been playing in a foursome against Noel and Georgie Vigors. I'd looked in on my way back from our Reading office. Holst and Mariner. I retired last year, but I still go in occasionally. As I was saying, I dropped by as the game was finishing and we all went in together for a drink. I gathered that Katie had intended to play with Jonathan, but he'd let her down at the last moment, and Walter had stepped into the breach. She was still annoyed about it. She didn't like people letting her down. And Walter isn't much of a hand at tennis, so they'd lost the game badly, which didn't improve her temper."

"She had a temper?"

"Oh yes. *De mortuis* and all that sort of thing. But she certainly had a temper."

"Please go on."

"All things considered, it was a bit unfortunate that Jonathan should have turned up at this moment, and not only turned up but turned up wearing flannels and looking as hot as if he'd been playing tennis himself. Katie said something like 'What's all this? I thought you were so busy putting your paper to bed that you couldn't play tennis,' and Jonathan said, 'That's right. It didn't take as long as I thought it would,' and Katie said, 'Wouldn't she cooperate?' and when Jonathan looked a bit blank she said, 'Your paper, I mean. When you put her to bed.' Everyone thought this funny, except Jonathan. He's not a young man who likes being laughed at. He said something fairly rude. I can't remember exactly what it was. Then they went at it hammer and tongs. It ended with Katie saying to Walter,

'You might run me home. I don't think I can stand much more of this ill-bred lout.' That broke the party up. We were all feeling pretty embarrassed, actually."

Knott seemed to be visualizing the scene, turning it over, shaking out any possible implications. He said, "Can you remember anything specific that was said when they were slanging each other? It might be important. You often get a lot of truth out of people when they're angry."

"I can't remember anything that was actually said."

"Who was angrier?"

"They were both angry, but Kate was definitely more in control of herself. She was able to pick her words and make them sting. Jonathan was out of control altogether."

"He sounds an unusual type."

Mariner drew a deep breath. O.K., here it comes, thought Knott.

Mariner said, "In my opinion, Limbery is a dangerous and unpleasant young man. You heard about the scene he made in church this morning?" Knott nodded. "That was absolutely typical. He has no control over his temper and very little sense of what is right and wrong. If you want an example of his outlook on life and morals I advise you to read some of the drivel he produces for his local rag. I've got some back numbers here. To me they're futile nonsense, although I suppose very young and immature people might be taken in by them, in which case I suppose they might be dangerous. Anyone with any sense just laughs at them." But Mariner wasn't amused, Knott noted. He was angry.

He said, "If you'd lend them to me I'll look through them. Do you think his violence is confined to words? Could it come out in actions as well?"

"Certainly it could. Last Christmas at a local dance Tony Windle was pulling his leg about one of those effusions of his and he took a swing at him. He picked the wrong man there. Tony's twice as quick as him and a bit of a boxer, too. He put him on his back."

"So what happened?"

"He scrambled up shrieking out a lot of filth and went for him again, quite unscientifically. But a lot of people had rallied round by then and he was pulled off and told not to be a bloody fool. I believe he apologized next morning. On the face of it, he and Tony are quite good friends. But I've noticed that Limbery hasn't graced any of our social gatherings since then—and thank goodness for it."

"He wasn't at the dance on Friday, I believe."

"That's right. Something about an article he had to finish. Though why there should have been any hurry for it I can't imagine. The Hannington *Gazette*'s a weekly rag, and comes out on Thursdays."

Knott said, "You don't like him very much, do you?"

"I don't like him at all," said Mariner. "There's no secret about that."

"So it's fair to assume that he doesn't like you."

"He dislikes everybody who's older than he is, or better off."

"Quite so. I wondered whether he might have been responsible for those stupid practical jokes I was hearing about. Letting down tires and emptying radiators and so on."

"Now that you mention it," said Mariner, "it's quite on the cards. When it started, we assumed it was kids playing jokes. But it could have been Limbery. That's his mental age."

"And one of his victims was Tony Windle."

"That's right," said Mariner thoughtfully. "So he was."

Old Mr. Beaumorris had once laid it down that, of all unnatural associations, the one to be most avoided was association between a parent and his married children.

Since Mr. Beaumorris rarely made any statement without a personal angle to it, it was assumed that he was talking about the household at Limpsfield, the ugly red brick house next door to the Croft, shared by the widowed sixty-one-year-old Vernon Vigors and his married son, Noel.

The house had been informally divided. Mr. Vigors senior regarded the rooms on the left of the front door as his private domain. He had furnished them to bursting point with pieces from a much larger house. The shelves were full of leather-bound books, and every available flat space held photographs and mementos of married life.

Knott had not found the old man informative. Forty years of solicitordom had accustomed him to asking questions, not to answering them. He agreed that he had left the dance at a quarter past eleven. He had driven straight home and had gone to bed. He had been practically asleep before his son and daughter-in-law had got home. He had no particular views about Katie. He thought she was a nice girl and failed to understand how anyone could have done such a thing to her, but supposed that they had to resign themselves to the fact that they lived in a violent age.

After twenty minutes of this sort of thing, Knott crossed the hallway to talk to the younger generation. The distance between them and the old man was three yards and thirty years. He found Noel and Georgie sitting together on the sofa in front of the open French windows which gave onto a small tidy garden. Since they had not left the dance until after half past eleven and could neither of them have had anything to do with the crime, he decided to question them together. In that way they would be able to supplement each other's impressions. He was particularly interested in the quarrel at the Tennis Club.

"I've been told how it started," he said. "Katie thought Limbery had stood her up. No girl likes that. But it doesn't sound like a reason for a public row. Particularly with someone you'd been rather attached to."

Noel and Georgie looked at each other. They could sense without difficulty the implications of what the Superintendent was saying

Georgie said, "Jonathan never minds his rows being conducted in public. It adds spice to them."

Noel said, "I think the heat was self-generating. One said one thing and that provoked a sharp answer. Both of them had saw-edged tongues, when they chose to use them."

"Can you remember what they did say? I don't mean the actual words. What line did they take?"

Noel said doubtfully, "It was a month ago—"

Georgie said, "Come on, Noel. You can do better than that. I remember perfectly well. When Katie got down to brass tacks, towards the end, she kept accusing Jonathan of being a schoolmaster manqué. A man among boys, a boy among men. That sort of thing. Immature. Trying to impress the kids but making a laughingstock of himself in the eyes of anyone who was adult. She said, 'You ought to rename that rag you run *Beezer* or *Tiger Tim's Weekly.*' "

"Yes. That's right. And he said that just because she couldn't understand anything more than the leading article in *Peg's Weekly* it didn't give her the right to sneer at *his* work."

"Something you said a moment ago, Mrs. Vigors. Schoolmaster manqué. Meaning he'd have liked to be a schoolmaster? Or that he'd tried it and failed?"

"Actually he did teach for a few terms at Coverdales. That was soon after he left school himself."

"Do you know why he stopped?"

Before Georgie could answer, Noel said, "Not really. No." He said it very firmly.

Knott's mind seemed to be running on schools. He said,

"Coverdales. That's at Caversham, isn't it? Just outside Reading. Boys and girls? Or boys only?"

"It was boys only when I went there," said Noel. "Now they take girls in the sixth form, for 'A' level subjects."

"Did Katie go there?"

"Good heavens, no," said Georgie. "That wouldn't have been nearly grand enough for the Steelstocks. She went to —What's the name of it? Princess Anne went there."

"Benenden."

"Right. I expect that's where she made a few friends who were useful to her when she got up to London."

"Friends are always useful," said the Superintendent.

While this was going on, Detective Sergeant Shilling was making an examination of the boathouse. The exterior of the doors had been dusted and had produced the expected number of fingerprints. The legible ones had been photographed. There was no reason to suppose that the murderer had touched the doors, but it was the taking of routine precautions, unnecessary in nineteen cases out of twenty, that characterized good police work.

The boathouse, he noticed, was built in two pieces. There was the main part, which housed boats and gear, a roomy single-story construction with an open penthouse at the back. On the west side, looking as though it might have been added as an afterthought, was a two-story annex. The big sliding doors which gave onto the ramp in front of the main section were padlocked, but there was a smaller door cut into the left-hand sliding door. It was in this that one of the panes had been broken. The jagged pieces had been carefully removed, and it was not easy at first glance to realize that the glass was missing.

Shilling put his hand through, reached downward and found the catch of the spring lock. He could just touch it with his fingers. He took off his coat, rolled up his sleeve and inserted his bare arm. This time the catch was in reach. He turned it gently and the door opened inward.

Not very secure, he thought. But since the most valuable items inside were the boats and since you would need to open the main doors to get them out, perhaps not dangerously insecure.

There were three smart-looking four-oar skiffs. The nearest, which had been recently varnished, had the letters G.C.M. in black paint on the stern. George Mariner? Alongside them, two tub dinghies and two rather shabbier skiffs. The rudders had been lifted out of their pintles and were stacked in a rack against the back wall. Just inside the door was a school desk, at which, no doubt, Mr. Cavey sat to record bookings. Behind this lay two canoes which looked as though they had had a hard life. The punts were moored along the landing stage, but would live under the penthouse at the back in winter. Punt and boat cushions were stacked in a neat pile under the window in the left-hand wall. Oars along the back wall, paddles, punt poles and boat hooks across the rafters. Everything shipshape and a credit to Mr. Cavey. The whole place smelled of hot varnish and creosote.

After a look around which produced no surprises, Shilling went out again, leaving the door ajar, and walked around to the side. The door of the annex was locked. Who would have a key?

Shilling went back into the boathouse and used the telephone which stood on the booking desk to call the Hannington police station. McCourt answered. He had spent two sweltering hours transcribing the tapes of his interviews with Roseabel Tress and the Havelocks.

He said, "Boat Club offices? Mariner will have one key.

But if I ask him for it he'll keep me waiting for at least half an hour. Jack Nurse is a better bet. He's secretary of the Boat Club. I'll nip up to his house on my moped and borrow it for you."

"I could do that," said Shilling. "I've got the car."

"No trouble," said McCourt. He welcomed the excuse to get out of the police station.

Sergeant Esdaile, realizing that Sunday was the rector's busiest day, had timed his movements so that he arrived at the Rectory at exactly two o'clock. He calculated that lunch would be over and Sunday School not yet begun. He had watched McCourt at work and was not looking forward to the labor of transcription. He planned to keep *his* interviews as short as possible. The rector had very little to tell him and seemed more interested in discussing Limbery's outburst in church. Esdaile headed him firmly back. He and his wife— Would the Sergeant like to have her in, too? Not necessary, said Esdaile—had walked back with the Group Captain and his wife to their house, the Old Rectory. He couldn't help thinking it odd that of all the money the Church Commissioners had made by selling these fine old buildings and housing the incumbents in bungalows, none had gone into increasing stipends.

"Scandalous," said Esdaile. "What happened next?"

"We had a cup of coffee. All except my wife, that is. She can't drink coffee at night. It keeps her awake."

"And what time did the party break up?"

"It must have been after midnight. You know what women are like when they start talking."

"And you walked home?"

"Certainly. It's only a very short distance. Past the Memorial Hall and the church. We noticed that Katie's car was still parked outside the hall and I think I commented

92

on it. My wife would remember. But of course, we neither of us had any idea—"

"Of course not, sir. Did you meet anyone? Did any cars pass you?"

"Let me think. No. We met no one and I don't think anyone passed us. The Street is very quiet at that time of night. I do remember that we heard a car coming down Brickfield Road. I said to my wife, 'I wonder who that is.' Just idle curiosity. And we stopped to have a look. You can see Brickfield Road from the Street. It's less than a hundred yards away."

"And did you recognize the car?"

"It was much too dark to recognize it. But we noticed one odd thing. It was driving on its sidelights. Dangerous, I should have thought. It was a dark night and there are no streetlamps in Brickfield Road, although it's not for want of asking. Young girls don't like walking down it at night . . ."

At this point Sergeant Esdaile slipped his hand into his coat pocket and switched off the tape. He had heard the rector more than once on the perils of Brickfield Road and knew that he was good for at least ten minutes on the subject of Youth in Dark Streets. He judged that if he got away by a quarter to three that would be about right for his visit to Jack and Sylvia Nurse.

"Nothing," said Sally Nurse. "Nothing happened at all. We went for a drive."

"Your mother and I were dreadfully worried."

"I've said I'm sorry. There wasn't the least need for you to be worried."

"A quarter past one! We were on the point of ringing up the police."

"They wouldn't have thanked you. They'd got other things to think about by then."

"*Anything* might have happened."

"The worst that could have happened," said Sally in an effort to lighten the discussion, "was that we might have turned the car over. Billy drives like a maniac."

Mr. Nurse was not to be diverted. He said, "In my young day, if girls went out for midnight drives with young men people knew what to think."

"Then people in your young day must have had filthy minds."

"Really, Sally. You mustn't speak to your father like that."

"Why not?" said Sally mutinously.

"Because he is your father."

"And I'm his daughter. And I'm nineteen, not nine."

"You're living in our house—"

"*And* paying for my keep."

"As long as you're living here, you've got to behave yourself properly."

"For God's sake," said Sally, her voice going up, "this is the twentieth century, not the reign of Queen Victoria. And it's England, not the Arabian Gulf. If you don't want me in the house, say so. I can find somewhere else to live—"

"Don't shout at me. I'm not deaf."

"I'm sure your father didn't mean—" said Mrs. Nurse and broke off.

Two policemen were coming up the front path.

NINE

"There's no need to be alarmed by this invasion," said McCourt pleasantly. "Sergeant Esdaile was on his way round to ask you a few routine questions. Lucky he's found you all together." He was looking at Sally as he spoke. He had heard the shouting as he came up the path. He thought that Jack Nurse must be a trying parent.

"All I'm here for," he went on, "is to borrow the keys of the Boat Club. Sergeant Shilling asked me to get hold of them."

"The keys," said Nurse vaguely. "Why?"

"I expect he just wants to have a look round."

"I suppose it's all right. I'll fetch them." He came back with two keys, each with a label attached. When McCourt had taken them and departed on his moped, Nurse said, "Do you want to question us together or alone?" He felt awkward about it. Sergeant Esdaile was a family man. He knew him and his wife well and had made their wills for them.

"You and your wife were together after the dance, so I gather," said Esdaile. "Save time if I had a word with you two first."

Sally took the hint and departed into the garden.

"There's not a lot to tell," said Nurse. "My wife and I left the hall soon after the Mariners. A minute or two after eleven, I should say. We walked straight home."

95

"Not a long walk," said Esdaile.

In fact their bungalow, *Syljack,* was almost directly across the road from the hall.

"Then we sat up and talked for a bit."

Mrs. Nurse said, "We watched the end of the film on television and had a cup of coffee to pass the time."

"To pass the time?"

"We never like to go to bed until Sally's back."

"When one o'clock came, we were very anxious. We thought we ought to do something. Then Sally came back, with Billy Gonville."

"That terrible car of his," said Mrs. Nurse. "You can hear it half a mile away. We asked her where she'd been and she said—"

"I'll ask her about that myself," said Sergeant Esdaile firmly.

One key said "Outer Door" and let them into a tiny hallway with a door on the left labeled "Committee Room" and a wooden staircase straight ahead. The air was heavy with stored heat and undisturbed dust. Like a forgotten attic in an old house, thought McCourt as he followed Shilling.

The committee room was unlocked. It was furnished with a table and chairs and two old-fashioned wooden filing cabinets. On the walls hung rows of framed photographs of regatta events. One was a photograph of a man with a large mustache, with the legend "Alfred Butt. Single Sculler. Oxford to London. Five hours, forty minutes." Mr. Butt had a thoughtful look on his face, as though he was wondering why he should have done such a thing. One of the cabinets held files of correspondence, membership cards and minute books. The other was empty. A moth flew out as Shilling opened it.

"No wonder they don't bother to lock it up," said Shilling. "Let's try upstairs."

The room upstairs was labeled "Chairman's Office." This was locked. The second of the two keys opened it. It had a square of carpet on the floor, a rolltop desk with a swivel chair in front of it, a small table and three wicker chairs. There was a triangular cupboard in one corner with glasses in it, a nearly full bottle of gin, a half-empty bottle of whisky and some unopened bottles of tonic and soda water.

"Quite a snug little den," said Shilling. "I suppose this is George Mariner's hideaway."

"He's a man who likes to do himself well," said McCourt.

This room had signs of recent use. There were three cigarette ends in a glass ashtray on the desk. They looked new.

"When was the last Boat Club Committee meeting?" said Shilling.

McCourt, after some thought, said, "I imagine it would have been in connection with the regatta. That was on July fifteenth."

"More than a month ago. They don't look a month old."

"He could have been up here dealing with correspondence. Something like that."

Before Shilling could pursue the matter they heard the telephone. It was ringing down in the boathouse.

"Wonder who that can be," said Shilling. "The Super's the only man who knows I was coming down here. Something must have turned up."

He made his way with no undue haste down the stairs. McCourt, left to himself, took a look around the room. The first object which struck his eye was the calendar on the wall beside the desk. The picture of the girl on it, if not actually obscene, came close to the borderline. McCourt's lips wrinkled in distaste. Two years as a policeman in London and three in the quieter backwater of Hannington had eradicated some, but by no means all, of the puritan ethos bred into him by his upbringing.

At that moment a small spotlight flicked across the room. It seemed to come from behind the desk. McCourt went across to examine the phenomenon.

He saw what had happened. When Shilling had opened the door to let himself back into the boathouse the sunlight, reflected off the glass, had shone directly onto the opposite wall. It had not only shone onto it. It had shone through it.

McCourt went down onto his knees behind the desk and found the hole. Originally a knothole, it looked as though it had been enlarged with a knife. As he knelt, it was on eye level and gave him a view of a section of the boathouse below. To the left he could see the legs of Sergeant Shilling, who was sitting at the chair behind the booking desk talking into the telephone. To the right the ends of the two canoes. Straight ahead, across the tops of the skiffs, he could see the flat punt cushions stacked in line under the window in the wall.

As he stared down through this peephole, other matters were circling through his mind, not settled yet into a definite pattern. The wheel marks of the car which had been parked farther along the towpath. The car which Roseabel Tress and the Havelocks had heard driving away at around midnight. The car which had aroused such a strong presentiment of evil in Roseabel's curious mind.

There was something else that one of the women had said to him. He felt sure that it was important. No need to trouble his mind about it. He could play back the tapes and listen. As he heard Shilling coming back up the stairs he scrambled to his feet.

"I've got to get back to the Steelstock house," said Shilling. "And pick up something on the way. At once, if not sooner. You'd better jump onto your moped and come too. Things are beginning to move."

"And I hope you're not going to be like Dad about this," said Sally Nurse.

"I've got two girls of my own," said Sergeant Esdaile. "They're only eight and ten. When they're a bit older, I expect I'll be exactly like your father. At the moment, I'm broad-minded."

"There isn't anything to be broad-minded about. Billy asked me if I'd like to go for a drive. You remember how hot it was on Friday night. I thought it was a chance to get a breath of fresh air before I went to bed." She smiled and suddenly looked much younger. "Oh, boy. Did I get some fresh air. We must have gone over a hundred down that bit of the motorway."

"Better give me a rough idea of where you went and what the timings were."

"Do my best," said Sally.

Esdaile let her talk, only interrupting her to say, "Yes. I heard about the police check. They had a lot of men out that night. It was organized from Reading. We weren't involved."

And later. "What did you talk about."

"What people always talk about, of course. We talked about ourselves."

"Did he . . . ?"

"If you're getting round to asking me if he tried to rape me, the answer's no. All he did was kiss me, in a brotherly way. Well, perhaps a bit more than brotherly. But he didn't paw me. He really is a very nice person."

"I'm sure he is," said Esdaile.

They had moved down to the far end of the garden but could hear the telephone when it rang. Mr. Nurse appeared and said, "It's for you, Sergeant. Superintendent Knott. He says it's urgent."

Knott's voice at the other end of the line was deliberately flat. He said, "Is Sally there?"

"Right here."

"Ask her to check if her evening bag's there."

"To check—"

"Just to check it. Not to open it. Not even to handle it. The bag she had with her at the dance."

Sally said, "What on earth! Why should he want that?"

"No idea," said Esdaile. "Suppose you go and look. He's hanging on."

"I expect it'll be in your bedroom," said Mrs. Nurse. She and her husband were listening to the conversation. "I didn't see it when I made your bed that morning."

"That's right. I remember I just threw it into one of the top drawers when I got back. There's nothing much in it."

"Could you see if it's still there. Don't open it. Just look."

"What does he think's in it, for goodness' sake?" said Sally. "A bomb?"

Mr. Nurse said sharply, "Don't be absurd. Just do what he asks."

Esdaile, still grasping the receiver, said, "I've no idea what it's all about. But could you just check on it."

Sally departed. The others stood in silence until she came back. They noticed she was looking upset.

"It's there all right. Where I said."

"Miss Nurse says the bag's here, sir. Just where she left it."

Knott's voice came over the telephone so clearly that everyone in the room could hear it. He said, "Good. Now listen. Do you know where Shilling has got to?"

"I expect he's still down at the boathouse. McCourt went down there with the keys for him. Less than half an hour ago."

"Is the boathouse on the telephone?"

Esdaile looked at Mr. Nurse, who nodded. The excitement was beginning to get hold of them.

"Right. I'll ask him to pick up the bag himself on his way past. I'm at Mrs. Steelstock's house."

He rang off. The four people in the room stood staring at each other.

TEN

The next person on Superintendent Knott's visiting list after he left Mariner's house had been Mr. Beaumorris, but, on reflection, he had decided to leave the old gentleman alone, for the time being at least. He could not really visualize him as having taken any part in the murder, since he had bicycled straight home from the dance and had sat until well after midnight in the bow window of his cottage in the street, seeing and being seen. He might be useful later as corroborative evidence of other people's movements.

There was a stronger reason for leaving him alone. The Superintendent knew that he disliked him and knew the reason for his dislike. He had not forgotten Bill Connington. He would certainly not be helpful and might even be obstructive. Knott therefore decided to go straight on to the Manor and talk to Mrs. Steelstock. She ought by now to have recovered from the initial shock and should be able to give him evidence on a number of points which were beginning to interest him.

West Hannington Manor was the oldest and incomparably the most handsome house in the village. Built in the reign of Queen Anne, it lay well back from the road, protected on three sides by an old brick wall and by ornate iron railings along the front. Matthew Steelstock, who had hated all modern inventions and had preferred a horse to a motorcar, had often expressed the intention of building a fourth and higher wall along the Street, but this had proved to be beyond even his purse and the project had died with him.

As the Superintendent walked up the drive he noted on his left, at right angles to the main building, the stable block, the end part of which Katie had converted into her private living quarters. He knew from his study of the plan that it had a private exit onto the lane on the east side of the property. It would have to be searched. He proposed to do this important job himself.

The door of the Manor was opened by a boy in corduroy trousers and a blue and white checked shirt. Peter Steelstock, said the card index in the Superintendent's mind. Sixteen. At Coverdales School. Wasn't at the dance. An immature nose, a band of freckles above it and the sullen look which seemed to be fashionable with boys of that age; it lightened when he smiled, as he did now. It was a smile which flicked on and off again as abruptly as a sky sign. Advertising something, or nothing? Difficult to tell at that age.

"You must be the Murder Squad," he said. "Mother's been expecting you. She's in the drawing room with Walter."

He led the way down a paneled passage into the big room at the back of the house which looked out over a wide stretch of lawn. It had been furnished with a real taste for its period, a taste which came from the widow, Knott guessed, and not from her late and unlamented husband, who seemed from all accounts to have been a Philistine as well as a bully.

Mrs. Steelstock was sitting upright on a wooden-framed tapestry-covered armchair. There was bone and character in that face. A lot of it had gone into Katie. Some of it into Walter. By the time they reached Peter, maybe the wells had been running low?

She said, "I expect the Superintendent wants to speak to me privately. He may want to talk to you afterwards."

When the boys had removed themselves, she indicated a chair for Knott to sit in and composed herself for questioning. A little too composed, perhaps, for a mother whose only daughter had been savagely killed less than forty-eight hours before?

She said, "Yes. Walter drove me home. I'm told by various people who have been busy checking other people's movements"—a slight smile touched her thin lips—"that we left at eleven twenty. I have no exact recollection of the time myself. When we got here I went straight to my room. Walter stayed up. He usually makes himself responsible for locking the house up."

"Would he have been waiting up for Kate?"

"No. Kate lived her own life. We didn't interfere with her in any way."

Lived her own life. Died her own death.

"I only wondered whether you could see her windows from this house. I mean, so that you would know, seeing lights go on, whether she got back."

"No. Her house is the far end of the old stable block. It used to be the coachman's cottage. It's completely hidden from the house. She preferred it that way."

"Was Peter up when you came back?"

The sudden switch did not disconcert Mrs. Steelstock. She said, "Peter was in bed. He had told us he had a headache. I think it was only an excuse. He's not of an age to find dances amusing."

103

"And you didn't wake him up when Sergeant McCourt came round with the news?"

"I discussed it with Walter. But there seemed no point in doing so. We told him next morning."

The Superintendent was not really interested in Peter. He had been devoting most of his mind to the question he had really come to ask. It had to be put in exactly the right way.

He said, "You'll understand that in a case of this sort— a girl being killed—the very first thing we have to consider is men who were . . . well . . . interested in her. In particular, I wanted to ask you about one of them. Jonathan Limbery."

"Yes?" said Mrs. Steelstock, her mouth set in a tight line.

"He was friendly with her?"

"At one time he was round this house so much that I got the impression he considered himself a member of the family. I appreciated that Kate didn't fancy entertaining him in her own little place. That would have been altogether too intimate. So she used to bring him in here. I really didn't know what to do with him. He hardly seemed to fit. Of course, there were things he could talk about. The firm Walter is articled to in Reading, Holst and Mariner, they happen to be the accountants for his paper. And he knew Peter. He'd taught him at one time at Coverdales. And he sometimes even condescended to talk to me, but since it usually developed into a lecture on politics or economics I can't say I found it very entertaining."

"But it was Kate he really came to see?"

"So I assumed."

"I'd be interested to know how he first got to know her."

"Sooner or later, Superintendent, in a place like West Hannington, everyone gets to know everyone else. In this particular case, of course, there was the song he wrote for her."

"Song?"

" 'What Are They Like in Your House?' "

"Good heavens! Did he write that?"

There had been a time, two or three years earlier, when you could hardly cross the street without hearing someone humming or singing or whistling the curiously seductive lilt: "What are they like in your house . . . your house . . . your house. Rich house . . . poor house."

"Kate used it as a sort of theme song when she started on television. I imagine the music publishers took most of the profits. They usually do, don't they?"

"So I understand."

"But it made a bit for both of them. I don't suppose Jonathan gets paid much for that stupid paper he plays at editing. I doubt if it sells a hundred copies outside this area. He uses it as a sort of pulpit for his views."

"Not very popular views?"

Mrs. Steelstock considered the point coldly. She was a curiously dispassionate woman, the Superintendent decided.

"Since they were mostly attacks on older people who were doing responsible jobs, they must have had a certain attraction for the young, I imagine."

A very faint echo flicked through the Superintendent's mind. Something he had overheard. It would come back if he didn't chase it. He said, "You'll have heard all about the quarrel Kate had with Jonathan at the Tennis Club."

"Certainly I heard about it. From the people who were there, and from a lot of people who weren't there but wished they had been."

"I'd appreciate your view of the reason for it."

"The reason?"

"People don't indulge in a public slanging match on the spur of the moment. They must have been building up for it."

"I think the reason was very simple. Kate had moved ahead of him. The fact that he was unsure of himself might have a certain appeal to young people who are unsure of themselves. But Katie was growing up. She was meeting people in London with adult minds. People who had really done something, not just talked about doing it. It was bound to alter her perspective."

"Anyone in particular?"

"If there had been some man, she would not have discussed him with me. We hadn't that sort of relationship. Of course there were girlfriends. People she was at school with, people like Venetia Loftus. Not Loftus now, of course. She's married. I forget the name."

Mrs. Steelstock smiled again as she mentioned this. She knew, and she knew that Superintendent Knott knew, that Venetia's father was the Assistant Commissioner in charge of Criminal Investigation at Scotland Yard: the man most directly responsible for Knott's professional future, the man whose influence had brought him so quickly to West Hannington and who would be watching the progress of the case with more than superficial interest.

Knott said, "Any men friends at all?"

"The only name I can remember being mentioned more than casually was Mark Holbeck."

"Her agent?"

"Yes."

"But he might have known if she had other close friends."

"He might," said Mrs. Steelstock. "But I think it was simply a business relationship." As the Superintendent got to his feet she added, with the first hint of personal feeling she had shown, "You will find the man who did it, won't you?"

"Yes," said Knott. "I'll find him." He opened his briefcase and took out the evening dress bag. "This was in the grass near Katie. I've no doubt it was hers, but I'd like you to identify it formally, please."

He stopped. Mrs. Steelstock had opened the bag and had started to examine the contents. Now he saw that her hand was shaking. He said, "I do apologize. I realize it must be painful for you—" and was interrupted.

Mrs. Steelstock said, *"This isn't Katie's bag.* She's never used lipstick of that color in her life. She couldn't. Anyway, I know the bag well. I gave it to her. I think I can tell you who it did belong to. Sally Nurse. She had a crush on Katie. Copied her clothes and everything." She stared at Knott, the horror beginning to build up in her eyes. "Do you think . . . Is it possible . . . My God, how cruel."

Knott, who was still trying to grapple with what had happened, stood staring at her. Then he said, "What do you mean?"

"That he made a mistake. That he killed the wrong girl."

"No," said Knott. "I don't believe that. But he certainly made a mistake. And if he did, he's going to pay for it a lot sooner than he expected. I'll have to use your telephone, please."

"Of course they think it's Jonathan," said Walter.

"Why should they?" said Peter furiously.

"Because he's the obvious person. He was keen on her. She turned him down flat. He's not the sort of person to stand for that."

"It's not true."

"How can you possibly know?"

"Because . . . because I know Jonathan better than you do. *And* I liked him. You and Mother hated him."

"That's a stupid thing to say," said Walter. "Why should we hate him?"

"No more stupid than saying Johnno would have killed Katie."

"All right," said Walter pacifically. Whenever Peter flew into a rage he found it easier to back down. "I'm not saying I thought he did it. I'm saying it's what the police will think."

The bags looked very similar, but when they were placed side by side on the drawing-room table in the clear afternoon sunlight, the small differences in the beading and metalwork were clear enough.

"I gather," said Shilling, "that Sally came home about one in the morning, had a flaming row with her parents, went up to her room, hurled this bag, which she thought, of course, was her own, into the drawer of her dressing table and hadn't touched it or thought about it again until you telephoned."

Knott seemed to be in no hurry to open the bag. He said, "You've read all the statements, Bob. And you can help us here, too, Mrs. Steelstock. I seem to remember that Katie had a chair fairly close to the main exit door. The one on the west side of the hall."

"I think that's right, sir."

"And that Sally Nurse had a chair close to hers. But even nearer to the door."

Mrs. Steelstock said, "Her chair would be as close to Katie's as she could possibly get it."

"So that it's perfectly possible that when Katie left in rather a hurry she picked up the wrong bag and took it with her. It partly explains one point that had been puzzling us. When we examined the bag we found near the boathouse we did notice"—Sergeant Shilling grinned at the use of the royal "we"—"that there were no keys in it. Since Sally had no car she'd need no car key. But she ought to have had a house key, surely?"

Shilling was about to say, "You don't know her parents," but realized that this was not a moment when comments would be welcome. Knott was talking deliberately because he was thinking deliberately, feeling his way step by step along the new and promising path which had suddenly opened in front of him.

He said to McCourt, who was standing unobtrusively near the door, "Find out, will you?" McCourt backed out into the hall and shut the door. Knott picked up Katie's bag, still without opening it, and said to Mrs. Steelstock, "I take it you identify this as your daughter's property?"

"Of course I do," said Mrs. Steelstock impatiently. "I told you. I gave it to her. Less than a year ago."

Knott clicked open the catch and upended the bag so that the contents slid out onto the table. Items of makeup, a handkerchief, some money and a ring with three keys on it. There was something else. Knott inserted a finger and thumb and drew it out delicately. It was a plain white envelope, which had been folded to get it into the bag.

Knott said, a note of savage satisfaction in his voice, "So *that's* what he was looking for."

"Then that's a note from . . . from the man . . . the one who got her to go down to the boathouse and—"

"That's right," said Knott.

"Aren't you going to look at it?"

"For the moment, what I'm going to do is label it." He took out a thin silver pencil and wrote on the envelope, "Taken from a bag identified by Mrs. Steelstock as belonging to Miss Steelstock." Then he initialed it, handed the pencil to Mrs. Steelstock and said, "You saw me take it out. Would you mind initialing it too."

She did so. Her fingers were clearly itching to extract whatever secret the envelope held. Knott took it back, still folded, placed it carefully in his wallet and put the wallet in the breast pocket of his coat.

McCourt reappeared. He said, "Sally did have a house key. And it was in her bag that night. But she didn't have to use it, because her father had the door open before she was halfway up the front path."

Knott considered this information, fitting it into the pattern which was forming in his mind. He said, "I take it your daughter was careful about locking up her house when she left it?"

"She's been careful since the burglary. Before that I don't think she bothered so much."

"Burglary?"

"About two months ago," said McCourt. "The man was actually in the house when she got back. Maircifully he seems to have been as frightened as she was. When he haird Katie coming through the front door he bolted out of the back. All she could tell us was that it was a man and youngish."

It was one of the difficulties of an investigation of this sort, thought Knott. Too much information. Important issues could become clouded by irrelevancies. As he thought about it he realized that everyone was looking at him. He smiled.

"Well," he said, "we'd better go down and have a look at her place ourselves. I'd like a word with Walter when we've finished. I wonder if you'd ask him to wait." Mrs. Steelstock nodded, but coldly. She was still angry that the Superintendent had refused to show her what was in the note. It had been found in her daughter's bag. It probably contained the name of her daughter's killer. Who had a better right to see it than her mother?

If Knott was aware of her displeasure he gave no sign of it. He led the way out of the house. His mood had changed. He was easy and, for once, talkative. It was the period of relaxation which follows a successful orgasm. He strode fast down the drive, toward the stable block, the sergeants almost trotting to keep up.

"It's making a lot of sense now, isn't it?" he said. "He was looking for that note. That's why he ransacked the bag. He didn't find it, of course. Because it was the wrong bag. *But he wasn't to know that.* His next idea must have been that Katie had left the note behind her in her house when she came out."

Shilling said, "I'd just about got that far myself."

"Right. So what does he do? He's a careful planner. But bold and quick when he has to be. I guessed that much almost as soon as I saw the body. *Now he thought he'd been given a second chance.* He'd take the key that was in the bag, thinking it was Katie's house key, and he'd come up later that night to have another look for the note. He'd be in a hurry, maybe a bit nervous. That's when mistakes are made."

Shilling said, "Let's hope so." McCourt said nothing. His deliberate Scottish mind was trying to keep up with this new and unexpected version of the Superintendent.

The coachman's cottage had been converted with tact. The only apparent addition was a two-story annex at the back. The rustic porch had been taken down and replaced by a plain strong door and the old windows taken out, the openings enlarged and modern frames put in.

Of the three keys on the ring from Katie's bag one was clearly a car key, one was a tiny cylinder of steel of the type known as a "Bramah." The third was an ordinary Yale. And it opened the front door for them.

Knott said, "He couldn't have opened the door with Sally's key. So let's try to find out how he *did* get in. Have a look round, Bob."

They waited, standing in the sunlight outside the open front door. Shilling reappeared. He said, "There's a window open at the back. It looks as if it's been forced. And I could see a chair that had been kicked over."

Knott grunted. He was trying, unsuccessfully, to see into the front room. He said, "We don't want three of us trampling about inside there. You go in, Bob. And open the curtains. Then we can see in."

They were heavy lined curtains and had been pulled right across the window. When they were drawn back, they could look in from the outside into what was evidently the living room. Shilling opened the window and said, "What do you make of that?" Against the wall, to the left of the window, was a desk. It was a solid affair, with drawers on either side of the kneehole and a cupboard on top of it. A masculine piece of furniture in a feminine room. The door of the cupboard had been forced. There was a gash in the woodwork beside the lock and a crack right across the panel.

"Rough work," said Knott. "Try the key."

He handed the key ring to Shilling, who moved across the room. McCourt noticed that he avoided standing directly in front of the desk, keeping over to the far side. The smallest of the three keys fitted the tiny keyhole.

"Not a lock he could pick," said Shilling. "So he bust it open. Using this, I shouldn't wonder." He pointed at the heavy steel poker lying in front of the fireplace, but he made no attempt to touch it.

"All right," said Knott. "Let's start the routine. Get Dandridge up here and warn him he's going to need help from Reading. We'll have the whole place dusted and photographed. Particular attention to the carpet in there, Bob. We want holograms of any footprints. When that's been done, have them take that cupboard door off its hinges, fit it up with clamps and a facing of cardboard or plywood—You see what I mean?"

"To protect the front surface."

"Right. And when you've got it rigged up, put it in the car. Tomorrow you can take it up to London when you go and hand it over to the boys at Hendon. And tell them not to take a month of Sundays about it."

"Quickest if I use the telephone here."

Knott thought about it and said, "Should be all right to use it. You come with me, Ian. We're going back to the house."

As they walked up the drive, McCourt could contain himself no longer. "Surely," he said, "the man would be careful not to leave prints. He'd likely be wearing gloves."

"Likely he would," said Knott with ferocious good humor. "And likely they'd be thin cotton gloves. And likely he wouldn't realize that on a hot night his hands would be sweating. You can sweat a fingerprint through cotton gloves. Did you know that?"

"I did not."

"It's not infallible. The camera has to screen out the mesh of the glove. But it can be done. And let me tell you something else, Ian, which may be useful to you later on." They had reached the doorstep of the house and the Superintendent paused with his hand on the knocker. "In a case like this you do *everything*. You take *every* step laid down in the book. Even when you know who the killer is."

McCourt gaped at him. During the last hour he had seen two different superintendents. This was a third. The father figure, dispensing wisdom to his children.

He said, "Did I hear you say, 'Even when you *know* who the killer is'?"

"Certainly. It was pretty clear all along what sort of man it had to be. We'll be putting a name to him in a few minutes. Knowing *who* it is doesn't really matter. It's a help, of course. But it's not the important point. We've got one problem and one problem only now. We have to put together a case that'll stand up in court." On the word "court" he thumped down the knocker. It was the full stop at the end of the sentence.

It was Walter who opened the door. Knott said, "Let's go in somewhere quiet." He indicated the dining-room door, on the left of the hall. Walter and Sergeant McCourt followed him in. He took his wallet out of his jacket pocket, opened it and extracted the folded envelope. He said to McCourt, "You've been with me, Sergeant, ever since I took this from Mrs. Steelstock and put it in my wallet."

"Aye."

"Then you are able to state that I haven't touched it until this moment." He turned to Walter. "And you can watch me open it."

"Certainly," said Walter. "But why—"

"Because," said Knott, "sooner or later, some snotty-nosed barrister is going to get up in court and say"—here Knott adopted a horrifically upper-class accent—" 'Naow, Superintendent, perhaps you will tell the court just haow you intend to prove that you faound this letter in the handbag of the deceased.' That's why I'm going to get both of you to initial this piece of paper which you see me extracting from this already identified envelope. Right?"

Walter said, "All right." McCourt said nothing. He felt breathless.

The Superintendent spread the paper delicately on the table, holding it by the edges. It was a plain sheet of white paper. They craned over Knott's shoulder to read the words which had been typed on it.

Darlingest Kit Cat. I can't keep this up a moment longer.
I don't believe you want to, either. If I'm not wrong
about that, come to our usual place. I'll be there at
eleven. LYPAH.

The Superintendent read it out loud, pausing on the last word, which was in capital letters. He said, " 'LYPAH.' That's an odd word. Do you think it's a name?"

He became aware that Walter was scarlet in the face. He was struggling with a mixture of embarrassment and laughter, in which embarrassment predominated. He said, "What's up, son? Something tickle you?"

Walter said, "It's LYPAH."

"You understand it?"

"It's just a stupid thing. It used to be a sort of catchword with some of the boys round here. I think it started at Coverdales, actually. You put it at the end of a letter—a letter like this—making a date with a girl."

"Why?"

"You put it there so that she'd ask you what it meant."

"I'm asking you."

"It meant 'Leave your pants at home.'"

The Superintendent considered this, but could think of no appropriate comment.

ELEVEN

"Then you're sure it came from Limbery," said Dandridge.

"Almost sure enough to prove it in court," said Knott. "Quite sure enough to make it a working hypothesis. The Steelstock boy confirmed to us that 'Kit Cat' was Limbery's pet name for Katie. He hadn't heard anyone else use it. The first part of the note indicates that they'd had a quarrel and he wanted to make it up. Well, we know all about that. And LYPAH. He'd have picked that nonsense up no doubt when he was teaching at Coverdales."

"In our part of the world," said Shilling with a grin, "we don't put LYPAH, we put—"

Knott said, "That's quite enough, Bob. We don't want any reminiscences of your lecherous past. There's a lot to do." He considered it, standing squarely on his stubby legs in front of the map in the operations room. Then he swung around on Sergeant Esdaile. He said, "I want a proper case book set up, Eddie. An hour-by-hour log of everything we've done and everyone we've questioned so far. Transcripts of what they said. A timetable showing people's movements that night. Copies of the photographs you took at the boathouse. Good photographs, by the way. I congratulate you. Photographs of the fingerprints on the boathouse door. Copies of Dr. Farmiloe's report and the report of the pathologist from Southampton. Also, as soon as it's available, a second report that I've asked for from Dr. Summerson, checking both of them. Not that I think there's anything wrong with them, but you can't be too careful with medical evidence. Then there'll be photocopies of this letter and a written statement, which I'll give you, of how and where it was found. You get the general idea?"

Esdaile looked dazed but resolute. He said, "You want everything we've got so far organized into one file."

"That's right. Next, we'll extend the search for the weapon. Have two men cover every yard of the way between the place where the body was found and Limbery's house. Search all drains, culverts, ditches and wasteland. We'll assume he wouldn't risk coming home via Upper Church Lane, because that would have taken him straight past the hall. He'd have stuck to the towpath, turned off it up Eveleigh Road and crossed the end of the street into Belsize Road. His house is number seventeen. That's just beyond the Brickfield Road crossing. It's the part they call Lower Belsize Road."

Dandridge said, "Windle and young Gonville share digs at number thirty-four Upper Belsize Road. They both say they heard Limbery's car coming back at sometime between half past one and a quarter to two. If he'd been out in his car, isn't it possible that he'd dumped the weapon miles away?"

"Extremely possible," said Knott placidly. "Even probable. Or he may have thrown it into the river five miles downstream. But killers do odd things. So we'd better make sure." He turned to Shilling. "You're going back to London. You know the points I want you to cover. You'll have a full program and I want you back tonight, so I suggest you take McCourt with you. He can do the checking at the Documents Division. It's in Lambeth Road. You can explain the form to him as you're driving up. Right?"

This seemed to be a signal for general dispersal.

The offices of the Hannington *Gazette* were fifty yards down East Street, on the south side. They occupied the ground floor and the yard of what had once been an undertakers' establishment. The editor before Jonathan Limbery had been an absent-minded man with a passion for wild flowers, on which he had written a number of booklets.

With the arrival of Jonathan, wild flowers had given way to wilder polemics, without noticeably changing the circulation figures. When Knott was announced, Jonathan was in his shirtsleeves, talking on the telephone. He said to the boy who had brought the news, "Find him a chair in the outer office. I'll give you a ring when I'm free," and continued with the call, which was to the news editor of the Reading *Sun.* It was a bad-tempered conversation, at least on Jonathan's part, which finished with him saying, "Even if you didn't use it, I think you ought to pay for it," and banging down the receiver.

After which he sat for a full minute, apparently deep in

thought, before stretching out his hand and ringing the bell.

"I can see you're busy," said Knott, "so I won't take up more of your time than I have to. As you probably know, we've been questioning everyone who was at the dance on Friday night when Miss Steelstock was killed. Now we're widening the scope of our inquiries to take in people, like yourself, who weren't at the dance but who were her friends . . . and acquaintances." Knott paused slightly before adding the last two words, then said, "Which category would you place yourself in, Mr. Limbery?"

"A friend," said Jonathan shortly.

"A close friend?"

"If you like."

"It's not what I like, sir. I'm just a poor dumb copper asking questions. Do I gather that you *were* a close friend?"

"Yes."

"A friend of the family?"

Came the faint flicker that Knott was trained to recognize. Without meaning to do so, he had touched a nerve. Follow it up.

He said, "I gathered from Mrs. Steelstock that you were quite a frequent visitor at their house—at one time."

"If she told you that, why ask me about it?"

"We like to have everything confirmed."

"Even though they haven't got a damned thing to do with the crime you're supposed to be investigating."

"You must leave it to us to judge that, sir."

"I can't stop you asking impertinent questions. I'm not bound to answer them."

"That's your privilege," said Knott. "Then perhaps we could deal with something which might be more relevant. You weren't at the Tennis Club dance?"

"No."

"Why not? All your friends were there."

"I don't have to account to you for my movements. Just take it that I don't like dances."

"A lot of us don't, sir. But wasn't there some other reason in your case? Some work you had to finish for your paper."

Jonathan looked up sharply, as though it had occurred to him for the first time that the Superintendent really had been doing his homework.

He said, "I don't know who told you that, but it happens to be true. There was an article I had to finish. And it was bloody lucky I did stay in. Otherwise I might have missed the fire."

"The fire?"

"Quantocks Paper Mills. Just outside Goring."

"Oh yes. I think I read about it. I didn't realize you'd covered that."

"I do a certain amount of local work for the Reading *Sun.*"

"I see, sir. A stringer."

"If you use technical terms, you should use them accurately. A stringer is an amateur. I am a whole-time professional newspaperman."

"My mistake," said Knott. "However, I take it you got a call from the *Sun* and volunteered to do them a piece."

"That is correct."

"At about what time?"

"It would have been around ten o'clock. I know that I was there by half past ten. When you're doing a piece for a daily, you have to keep an eye on printing times."

"Of course, sir."

"They put the paper to bed at one o'clock, so anything I did give them would have to be dictated over the telephone."

"And that's what you did, sir?"

"Yes."

119

"At what time?"

"Around midnight. Perhaps a little later."

"And where would that have been from?"

"From a call box on the Oxford road. Come to think of it, it must have been a little before midnight, because I had time for a quick drink and a sandwich at the King of Clubs. That's that big roadhouse between Goring and Whitchurch—"

"I know it well," said Knott, with a smile. "I've often dropped in there myself. A nice place. Broad-minded about closing times, too, I found."

"I think they had a Friday night extension." Knott noticed that Limbery was much easier now. "Anyway, they weren't in a hurry to turn me out. It must have been nearly half past twelve before I left."

"And came back home the same way."

"Actually, no. There's not a lot in it, but the King of Clubs is a bit closer to Whitchurch than it is to Goring. So I came back that way."

The Superintendent seemed to be visualizing the map. He said, "Wouldn't that mean you had to go all the way back to Reading to cross the river?"

"Certainly not. There's a bridge between Whitchurch and Pangbourne."

"Of course. Stupid of me. So that's the bridge you used?"

"Right."

"And were home by when?"

A shade of caution was observable in Jonathan's voice as he dealt with this question. He said, "I wasn't keeping one eye on my watch the whole time, Superintendent."

"Naturally not, sir. But we can work it out roughly, can't we? I take it you came straight back. You didn't stop for any reason?"

"No."

"And you'd left the roadhouse by half past twelve."

"Now I come to think of it," said Jonathan slowly, "it must have been even later than that."

"What makes you think that?"

"I remember now. When I was driving through Pang-bourne, I saw the clock on the Town Hall. It was a few minutes before one."

"Then it's about twelve miles to Hannington. Say twenty-five minutes. That gets you home at twenty past one."

"I don't drive fast at night. It might have been any time between half past one and two."

If the Superintendent observed the way in which the timing was stretching, a little implausibly, toward two o'-clock, and so matching itself with the statements made by Windle and Gonville, he gave no sign of being disturbed by this. He said in his smoothest voice, "Quite right to be careful at night. Why did you stop visiting the Manor, Mr. Limbery?"

Jonathan's head jerked around. There was a moment of silence. Then he said very softly, "Would you mind repeating that?"

"I asked, Why did you stop being a regular visitor at Hannington Manor?"

"I thought that's what you said. I've no intention of answering the question."

"Was it because you'd quarreled with Miss Steelstock?"

Jonathan said nothing.

"I was referring, of course, to that little tiff you had with her at the Tennis Club—about six weeks ago, wasn't it?"

Jonathan had started breathing deeply, taking in great gulps of air. It reminded Knott of a diver charging his lungs with oxygen before a deep plunge. He said, "I only mention it because it seems to have been fairly common knowledge. After all, if you conduct your quarrels in public, people are bound to talk about them. But what puzzled me was why it should have made you drop Mrs. Steelstock and her boys. Like I said, you were a friend of the whole family."

Again that flicker. Keep at it.

"That's right, isn't it, sir?"

"I realize now," said Jonathan, in a voice so thick with fury that the words had some difficulty in forcing their way out, "exactly what people mean when they talk about police harassment."

"Oh, come, sir. A perfectly straightforward question."

"You've no more right to question me about my personal relationships than I have to question you about yours. Suppose I started asking you impertinent questions about your wife and your girlfriends—"

"There's a difference. My girlfriend, supposing I had one, doesn't happen to have had her head smashed in."

But Jonathan was hardly listening to him. A dangerous and explosive mixture was building up inside him, a mixture of which he hardly understood the elements himself. Contempt for his father and resentment of his authority. Building from that, resentment of the authority of old people over the young, of employers over employees, of the conventional over the unconventional, of the state over its subjects—all personified in this sly and bullying policeman.

The lava belched out, scalding and stinking, but pleasurable to the god of the volcano. He said, "I loathe you and I despise you. You're a puffed-up nothing. A sadistic little bastard. We've all heard about you. How you like tormenting helpless and frightened people. I'm not helpless and I'm not frightened of you, or twenty like you. And I'm glad to answer for everyone you've trampled over in your filthy bullying life who've been too timid to answer for themselves. I've only one message for you. And that is Fuck off.

122

Crawl back down whatever hole you came out of and leave us alone."

Knott said, without a flicker of expression, "I ought to warn you, sir, that everything you say is being recorded."

Limbery hardly seemed to hear him. He was still inflated by the passion of his own rhetoric. He said, "Tell your superiors. Tell the world. The sooner people realize what they're up against, the better. We point our finger at other countries, but we can't see what's happening here. This is a police state. A filthy fascist police-ridden autocracy."

"Well now," said Knott, "all countries have got to have policemen. After all, there has to be someone to direct the traffic."

If Jonathan had been less exalted by the wind of his own oratory he might have detected the purring note of satisfaction in the Superintendent's voice.

TWELVE

During his service in the Metropolitan Police, McCourt had visited the headquarters of the Forensic Science Laboratory at 109 Lambeth Road on a number of occasions but had never before penetrated as far as the Documents Division, which occupied part of the fourth floor.

A notice beside the lift regretted that it was temporarily out of order "owing to maintenance work" and he resigned himself to climbing the flights of stone steps.

It was three years since he had quit the shabby, crowded, jostling streets of London for the peace of Hannington.

He was a country boy. His father was a Scottish Unitarian minister and his mother the daughter of an Oxford don, so he and his two sisters had been brought up in a house where intellect was treasured and integrity was more than a catchword. It had been planned for him that when he left Glasgow High School he should go to the university and study law. The death of his father when he was eighteen had killed this project. His mother had uprooted the family and moved back south to be near her own folk. It was at this point that Ian had made up his mind. If the academic study of the law was now out of his reach, he would pursue it on its executive side. He had joined the Metropolitan Police as a constable.

The stairs he was plodding up now were no harder than some of the steps he had climbed in those years, but serious application to the job in hand, backed by his educational standards, had won him a place at Bramshill and the early promotion to sergeant for those who survived the course there.

It was an unhappy chance that his first C.I.D. posting should have been to West End Central.

Ian McCourt was a natural puritan. Some of the sights he had seen and some of the things he had to do in London's square mile of vice had sickened his simple soul. When things had come to a head and he had been offered the chance of transfer to the Berkshire Force, he had jumped at it. He would not only be back in the country. He would be closer to his mother, who needed him now that her daughters had married and gone.

One more flight. He was glad to note that he was hardly out of breath.

It was the arrival of Superintendent Knott which had upset him. He had recognized in him a hard professionalism, an ideal which he had once held himself and which was now slipping out of his reach in the backwater of Hannington.

Mr. Mapledurham, the head of the Documents Division, had been warned to expect him. He examined the photocopy of the letter with expert attention, scratched the back of his neck and said, "A Crossfield Electric, I should say. Not a golf ball, though. The earlier mark."

Ian tried to look intelligent.

"A lot of machines are turning to the golf-ball type now. It might be an Olympia or a Hermes, but I don't think so. We can easily find out. Let's see what we've got. Short 'm' and 'w.' Serifs at top *and* bottom of the 'I.' Lateral at the bottom of the 'T.' That should be enough to be going on with."

Remembering Knott's instructions, McCourt said, "How long will it take?"

"Ten minutes, if the line's clear."

"Ten minutes?"

"That's right. We'll put it on the computer." He was scribbling out a message as he spoke and said to the young man who sat at the other desk, "Feed this into the magic box, would you, Les. Gent wants an answer quickish."

"I'd no idea," said Ian. "I imagined these things took weeks to work out."

"Some things take months. Some things take minutes. That's science for you. If it'd been a Ransmeyer we'd have had a lot more trouble. That's a communal type face, used by a lot of different machines. I'd guess this is a PLX face, which generally means a Crossfield."

"Will it make it easier, or less easy, if it does turn out to be an electric machine?"

"It won't make any difference in identifying the machine. Make it more difficult to peg it down to any one typist. With a manual machine you get variations in

125

pressure. An electric machine smooths them out."

"But if I got hold of another letter typed on this machine, you'd be able to say for certain that they both came from the same machine? Sorry. That was a bit confused, but you see what I mean."

"I see what you mean and the answer's yes. Provided the two samples were typed reasonably soon after each other. Machines develop different peculiarities as they grow older."

"Like people," said Ian.

Soon after that Les came back and said, "You're right. It was a Crossfield Mark Four Electric."

Mr. Mapledurham was consulting a large book. He said, "Crossfield Mark Four. Ex-factory at the end of 1973. Available in the shops early in 1974. I'll make one guess about your machine. It doesn't come from an office. If it had been bashed by an office typist for several years the type face would be a lot more worn. Anyway, this letter wasn't typed by a professional."

"How can you tell?"

"Spacing and alignment. If you wanted a guess, I'd say a private owner. Someone who did a fair amount of typing, but not a professional."

"Thank you," said Ian. "That's going to be very useful."

"Do you want a written report?"

Ian thought about Superintendent Knott and said, "Yes. I'm afraid we shall want a written report. I'll give you the address."

Mark Holbeck's agency occupied the third floor of an eighteenth-century house in Henrietta Street, Covent Garden. It looked across at the Tuscan portico of St. Paul's Church, designed by Grinling Gibbons, from which Samuel Pepys had watched a Punch and Judy show and in which Professor Higgins had met Eliza Doolittle.

Mark Holbeck was a young-old man with a sunburned and freckled bald patch in the middle of an outfield of sandy hair. If you asked what he did for a living he would tell you that he dealt in words and flesh, which meant in the jargon of his trade that he promoted both books and people.

The books were all around him, new copies in bright jackets. They filled every shelf in his office, spilled over onto the floor, occupied the window seats and trespassed onto his table. He shifted a couple off a chair and waved to Shilling to be seated.

"Of course I read all about it," he said. "It was in the later editions of the Saturday papers, and the Sunday papers made a meal of it."

First surprise. Lack of any real evidence of distress.

Shilling said, "She was your client. I imagine it must have come as a considerable shock to you."

Holbeck looked at him with the suspicion of a smile. "Sorry, Sergeant," he said. "No crocodile tears. Naturally I don't approve of people who kill my clients. It costs me ten per cent of their annual earnings. And in Katie's case that was beginning to add up to a very respectable sum of money. But no personal involvement."

"I wasn't suggesting anything of that sort, sir. I was just surprised that you didn't seem to mind much. On a personal level, I mean."

The two men looked at each other. Each was sizing the other up. Holbeck said, "What are you after, Sergeant? An analysis of her character or a list of her friends?"

"Both might be helpful, sir."

"I'll do what I can for you, on one condition."

"Yes, sir?"

"That you stop calling me sir. It's a habit policemen seem to have picked up from watching television."

Shilling grinned and said, "O.K. It's a deal."

"All right then. I first met Katie when she was eighteen. She had just left a top-line girls' school and wanted to behave like all the debby friends she'd made there, but she realized that she hadn't quite got the money to do it. Only two choices. She had to make money or marry it. And there were quite a few men—old men"—Holbeck's mobile mouth wrinkled at the corners—"who were prepared to buy her, even at the price of matrimony. She was sensible enough to say no. And she started out on the other route. She had no acting experience, so it was tough going. She got a job as a researcher with one of the independent television companies. A producer who liked her looks—correction, who liked her—wangled her a spot in one of their advertising quickies. And it *was* a wangle. He'd have had to get round Equity rules, but he did it. That was the beginning."

Holbeck stopped. He was looking back seven years, and some of the things he was seeing seemed not to please him.

He said, "You need just one quality to succeed in that field. It isn't beauty and it isn't brains, though both are useful. It's a rock-hard, chilled-steel determination to succeed. You asked me just now if I liked Katie. I didn't like her. But I respected her. One day—it was after she'd been working for about two years and making peanuts out of it —Rodney Ruoff the photographer made an approach. Through me, of course. I'd been half expecting it. Katie was playing down her age in those early commercials. Down to fourteen or even younger. Girls with small bones and unextravagant figures can go on doing that for a surprisingly long time. Rodney was very interested in young girls. And boys. He's known in the trade as 'Rod the Sod.' He's also a brilliant photographer and really has got some sort of pull with the television studios. Katie knew all about him. She asked my advice. I said, 'Steer clear of him. He's dangerous.' She said, 'If I was able to handle you,